GREEK RANSOM

MICHAEL MALAGHAN

ANDERSEN PRESS • LONDON

First published in 2008 by
ANDERSEN PRESS LIMITED,
20 Vauxhall Bridge Road, London SW1V 2SA

www.andersenpress.co.uk

British Library Cataloguing in Publication Data available

ISBN 978 184270 786 9

Typeset by FiSH Books, Enfield, Middx.
Printed and bound in Great Britain by CPI Cox & Wyman, Reading, Berkshire

CONTENTS

For Caroline:
with whom I discovered
the Mycenaean Tombs at Mazarakata,
one sunny afternoon in Greece.

1

NIGHT CRAWLER

Callie Latham was swimming in the crystal blue sea off the Greek island of Thelta. She paused in the water to move a strand of dark wet hair from her eyes.

She thought she might swim a little further. A finger of black rock was pointing out into the sea, and she wanted to know what was on the other side. Maybe there was a hidden cove, or a ruined Greek temple. Callie struck off with a confident crawl stroke.

She had been swimming for another five minutes when – CRUNCH! Something had grasped her by the legs, and was dragging her under. Callie kicked against it, and thrashed her arms, but she was being carried deeper still. Unseen hands were crushing her waist and her chest, squeezing the breath from her. It was as if a whole army of hands were tugging at her.

Callie thought of octopus and squid, but she could see nothing, nothing at all. What gripped her was the very water itself, and it was sucking her deeper, its hold getting stronger and stronger as her struggles became weaker.

The last of the air escaped from her mouth in bubbles as she instinctively cried out for help. She had spent her final breath futilely. No one would hear an underwater scream. No one would come to rescue her.

*

Thelta, One year later.

'It's that way,' Callie's brother announced, pointing off in completely the wrong direction.

He was a year younger than Callie, less than an inch shorter, and a complete pain in the neck. He was blue eyed and had annoyingly blond hair, finding him much favour with the locals (unjustified, as far as Callie was concerned). In Greek lore, blond children were blessed by the gods. His name was Nick.

'How can it be? We've just come from that way.'

Nick screwed up his face. 'Are *you* sure?'

'I tell you what – you go back that way and I'll go this way.'

'Getting a bit stressy, aren't you?'

'Yes!'

Callie was walking as fast as she could. They were getting more and more lost in the Greek wilderness, and the daylight was fading rapidly. In the last fifteen minutes it had gone from comfortingly light to alarmingly dark, and the view still looked the same in every direction – bleached grass, sunburned earth and dry rocks.

A cricket landed on Callie's bare leg and she gave a startled cry and dashed it away with her hand. The crickets seemed to be at their most active at night, their harsh call like fingernails down an old blackboard. Callie wished she could see where she was walking. There were lizards out here, and even worse, snakes.

'What was that?' Nick sounded scared.

Callie had heard it too. It was an unearthly scream, not quite human and not quite animal. In the darkness, Callie wasn't even sure which direction it had come from, or, how close it was. 'I don't know,' she whispered, not sure she wanted to.

The sound came again. Only this time it was a roar, echoing on the wind. Callie wanted to run. But which way? Which way was Limani, the village where they were staying? *Limani* meant harbour. All they had to do was find the sea! 'Come on. Maybe it's a bit further on.'

Callie's uncertain footsteps led them along a rise and suddenly, miraculously, she could see the sea: indistinctly, yet a marker as to where they were.

'Look,' Callie pointed to a small black island, a little out to sea. 'Skatelios Island.' It was right in front of where they were staying.

She started to run down the dark hillside, imprinting the impression of Skatelios Island into her mind in case the sky blackened further and she lost sight of it.

This time the inhuman cry was closer. It sent ice through Callie's veins. She faltered. They were running straight for the sound, when every instinct said they should be running away.

'What *is* it?' whispered Nick, keeping much closer to Callie than usual. 'It, it, sounds like a ... *lion.*'

Callie could not answer. It was a sound which belonged to rage and cruelty, and it *did* sound like a lion. Something out there was hunting, she was convinced of it. But what, or who, was it hunting in the Greek night? Callie wondered what to do. Should they go on, or were they headed straight into danger? Before she could make up her mind, a figure pounced out of the darkness – straight at them. Callie froze.

'Callie, Nick? Is that you two?'

'Dad?' Callie heard the relief in her own voice.

'I've been looking all over Thelta for you!' Their dad came jogging up. He looked more like a surfer than what he really was – an archaeologist who specialised in Ancient Greece.

'We got lost...'

'What did I tell you about how quickly the night comes down here?' He turned on his heel and started leading them back down the hill, in the same direction the screams had come from.

'Dad, what was that roaring noise?' asked Callie.

'It sounded like a *lion*,' added Nick.

Callie felt her dad's arm around her shoulder. 'It's from that little island out there' – he nodded towards the dim shape of Skatelios Island – 'so we're probably safe.'

'But what *is* it?'

Her dad shook his head. 'No idea...Now come on. You two are going straight to bed when we get back.'

'Straight to bed! But it's really early!' complained Nick.

'Bed!' repeated Callie's dad. 'Mum and I have to study some new Mycenaean finds tonight...so end of.'

'Mycenaeans! Mycenaeans! Mycenaeans!' mumbled Nick. 'It's always Mycenaeans!'

One last inhuman scream echoed across the sea.

*

Callie realised she was in King Akanon's Palace, on Mycenaean Thelta, and the year was 1270 BC. She was dreaming again. So often her dreams took her to the past, and brought to life the words she'd read in a book. And sometimes her dreams went far beyond the words. They were echoes in time.

'To war! To war!'

The war trumpets, curved like elephants' tusks, were blaring loudly and intermittently, like the braying of nervous sheep. Slaves were running, burdened with armour, shield and spear. Women were wailing and prostrating themselves on the marble floor.

Brightly coloured frescoes covering the walls of the palace depicted warriors and scenes of battle. Soon there would be more images of warfare: King Akanon and his army had been commanded to take ship and join the mightiest fleet ever assembled. King Agamemnon, King of all the Mycenaeans, would make war upon the Trojans.

Callie knew that her parents would have given anything to be where she was now. They had spent their lives searching for King Akanon.

He was striding confidently beside Callie. He was taller than she was, and at twelve, the same age. He seemed much fitter than other boys her age and surprisingly at home with the sword he carried. His jaw was set in a grim line of determination, his hair a long golden cascade.

Callie realised they were walking down a long set of steps, glazed with small oblong tiles the colour of midnight blue, and through a stone gateway with a bronze lion sitting on either side.

Two sentries built like champion body builders stepped aside for their young king.

'We're going to the Royal Treasury,' thought Callie. Her parents had been seeking the lost Treasury for years.

'We must guard our wealth against the thief who would take advantage of our absence.' King Akanon's voice was not deep, yet full of confidence and maturity.

He had stopped in a giant chamber, which was undecorated and unadorned, merely sandstone block walls reaching ten metres high, and in the middle of them, the largest bronze doors in all the Mycenaean world.

How Callie wished she could see inside. She had read of a truly breathtaking treasure: gold in coin and jewellery, gold plates and drinking vessels, masks of Akanon's royal ancestors, armour and shields, Akanon's golden throne, battle chariots decorated with gems. And the royal barge, a ceremonial ship sheathed in the precious yellow metal and inlaid with polished crystals: topaz, sapphire and azurite – the many blues of the Aegean Sea.

There was a mighty clunk, followed by a second and a third, as three great keys locked the portal to incalculable wealth.

The three keys were being drawn from the locks by the most trusted of Akanon's royal guard. Each man had protected their lord and king since his birth. Their loyalty was unquestionable.

'Ride out,' King Akanon commanded them now, 'and

return the keys to the three secret places I have made.'

Callie felt a thrill of excitement. Men had searched for more than three thousand years for the lost keys of Thelta; her mum and dad had made a film about it for the BBC.

The three guards bowed and were gone. King Akanon beckoned to someone.

His sister, the Princess Electra, tiptoed forward. Callie blinked. It was like looking into a mirror: Princess Electra was her double!

Akanon led his sister to a table. 'Here is the map.'

Four carved clay tablets made up a map in jigsaw-puzzle form, the interlocking pieces forming a triangle, the same shape as Thelta. The corners of the map locked together with one centre piece and the whole was no bigger than the red triangular warning signs outside Callie's school gates saying 'Beware Kids!' The entire surface was crisscrossed with intricate markings and symbols.

Akanon pointed at the clay map with his sword. 'Drawn by my own hand. No soul on earth will find where the keys to the Treasury are hidden unless they have all four segments of the map. Only when I am safely out at sea shall I send word of where all can be found. This is for your safety – for all on Thelta shall believe I take the secret with me to Troy.'

'But why should I need the map or the keys?' asked the Princess tremulously. From the redness around her eyes, Callie guessed she had been one of those women she'd heard crying, lamenting the court's preparations for war.

'For if I should fall at the gates of Troy,' Akanon said gently. He gave Electra a quick hug and the embarrassed grin that boys his age give their sisters. 'But it'll never happen. We take a fleet of one thousand ships. No power in the world can prevail against us.'

Princess Elektra pummelled him. 'Just make sure you don't do anything brave.'

'I promise, Little Princess.'

Callie looked up suddenly. The war trumpets were braying again.

King Akanon was heading for the lion-guarded doorway. 'One last word, my sister: let it be known what happens to any who should open my royal treasury without the keys.'

'What . . . ?' asked the Princess in a tiny voice.

'BOOM! The whole vault will fall upon them like pillars in an earthquake.'

BOOM!

Callie awoke with a start.

I'm still dreaming, she told herself but then the noise came again: quite distantly. It was more like a rumble of thunder, only this thunder was not in the sky. It was beneath her feet.

'Finally! We're going to get an earthquake.' Nick had marched right into her bedroom without knocking. 'What's the point of going on holiday where they get earthquakes if you don't have one?'

'Maybe we'll both get buried alive under tons of rubble,'

said Callie sarcastically. 'Wouldn't that be exciting!'

She looked around her room for her mobile phone and the rest of her things. If this really *was* an earthquake, they should be getting out of the villa. Where were her mum and dad anyway? Shouldn't they be doing something?

Nick seemed to have come to the same conclusion. 'I'm going to get Mum and Dad up.'

Callie was left alone. She listened, but the rumbling seemed to have stopped. When she thought about it, that's all it had been – just a rumbling noise; no trembling of the earth, no shaking of the floor beneath her bed. An earthquake! Why did she even *listen* to her brother? She loosened the sheets which were sticking to her, and turned over to go back to sleep.

'You'll never guess what!'

Nick was back again.

'It's a volcano?' groaned Callie sleepily.

'Mum and Dad aren't there.'

Callie pulled the sheet over her head. 'Go back to bed.'

'Honestly – they're not there.'

Callie switched on her bedside lamp. 'If this is one of your jokes, Nick, you're going to find out what it's really like to be in an earthquake.'

Callie climbed out of bed shivering in just her purple cotton pyjamas.

Her bedroom and Nick's were on the first floor of the villa, their parents' was above them on the second floor. Callie followed Nick upstairs, the marble steps cool under her bare feet.

The door to their parents' bedroom stood open. Callie hesitated on the threshold but Nick was already inside and throwing on the light. Now they'd really be in trouble. But the room was deserted, the bed pristine and unslept in.

'Where are they?' demanded Nick, as if Callie were privy to secret information.

'How should I know? I thought you were making it up...Mum...Dad...' She knocked on the adjacent bathroom door before opening it. It was dark – and devoid of parents.

'Maybe they're in the kitchen or the lounge,' she suggested.

'At three in the morning?' snorted Nick, but Callie noticed he still followed her back downstairs.

The kitchen and the lounge were empty too. Amongst the clutter and discarded clothes on the dining table, Callie found her mum's mobile phone. 'No point phoning her then.' Dad's mobile had packed up a week ago and he still hadn't got it fixed.

Callie flicked the switch that operated the outdoor security lights, and opened the door. The harsh sound of chirruping crickets greeted her. She listened hard for a minute but the inhuman cry they'd heard before seemed to have stopped.

'Stay inside, Nick.'

'Yeah! Like that's going to happen! I'm coming with you.'

For once, Callie didn't mind him getting his own way.

She stepped into a pair of flip-flops and led the way outside.

Stone steps led down to a patio and a carport. The black four-by-four jeep was still parked there. They couldn't have gone far then.

Callie walked to the rear of the villa. The surface of the oval swimming pool was glittering under the outdoor lights. There was a slight humming noise from the villa's generator, which was housed in a small underground bunker built nearby.

'What are you looking for?' whispered Nick.

'I don't know,' Callie admitted. What *was* she looking for: her parents swimming, moon bathing, or something suspicious? Villa Limani looked the same by night as it did by day: light coloured walls under a terracotta roof, with balconies extending from the bedrooms, and pretty, shuttered windows facing the nearby sea.

'They must be on the beach,' said Nick.

Callie pulled a face. 'Why must they?'

Nick shrugged. 'To beat the rush?'

Callie rolled her eyes and glanced at the sea, inky blue in the moonlight. There was the merest glimmer of light opposite Limani beach, where Skatelios Island appeared to float on the sea. She listened again and was relieved not to hear any inhuman cries from across the water.

Nick gave out a sigh. 'Well, they're not here. Let's go and look for them on the beach.'

'No way! I'm not getting lost again.'

Callie pushed Nick back indoors. She locked the door

behind them and wandered into the lounge. She flung herself onto the sofa. 'Well, I'll never get back to sleep now.'

'What do you think's happened to them?' asked Nick. 'Do you think that howling thing's got them?'

'No.' Callie felt annoyed. 'Why would they go out and leave us on our own?' She was facing the patio doors where a thin, floaty green curtain was pulled across. A shadow fell onto it as somebody walked past outside.

'They're back,' she said, and ran to the window to see which direction they were coming from. She fell back with a short scream.

'What's the matter?' Nick was staring at her.

'Someone's creeping about out there and it's NOT Mum and Dad.' She'd seen him in the security lights. Her impression was of an overweight man, sneaking around the side of the villa. She didn't think he'd seen her.

'Yeah! Nice try.' Nick didn't believe her. There was a sudden rattle as someone tried the patio door. Nick spun round. 'It's someone trying to break in!'

Callie shook her head uncertainly.

'The police! We should call the police,' Callie whispered, as the shadow moved away from the door. She picked up her mum's mobile phone and stared at the screen in dismay.

Nick mouthed the word, 'What?'

'I've no idea what the number is.'

'Try nine nine nine.'

Callie keyed in the number she would have used at home. Nothing happened. She threw the phone down in disgust.

She wanted to look out through the window again but was too scared. If the night crawler realised there were only two kids in the villa he might—

Callie and Nick twisted round together.

'He's trying the side door!' gasped Nick.

Callie suffered a clutching pain in her stomach, trying to remember if she'd re-locked it. Then, yes, she knew she had.

She tiptoed to the hallway, and peered at the door. It was still firmly shut. She heard another noise – somebody treading on a metal grate. There was one at the front of the villa, and the man looking for a way in had stepped on it. Callie took a sharp intake of breath as she heard something hitting the window.

'He's not going to go away!' said Nick.

Callie stared at a large bunch of car keys on the table. 'Do you remember Dad showing you how to drive the jeep?'

Nick looked surprised. 'Yeah.'

'Do you think you could do it now?'

'Yeah, but *he's* still out there!'

'He's at the front and the jeep's at the back.'

Nick swallowed and then nodded. 'Okay.'

Callie ran to the patio doors and carefully moved the curtain back a few centimetres. 'Unlock the jeep with the remote from here, and then make a run for it.'

Nick nodded and aimed the car key at the black jeep.

Callie operated the latch on the patio door and slid the glass panel aside. 'Now!'

Nick pressed the key. The jeep made an answering bleep and all the indicators flashed on and off again. They sprinted across the patio and leapt in, slamming the doors behind them. Nick stabbed the car key again to lock them inside. Then he was fumbling the key into the ignition. A man came running round the corner of the villa.

'It's Night Crawler! He's heard us,' shouted Callie.

2
GLASS EYE

Nick somehow managed to ram the key into the ignition and turned it the way their dad had shown him. The engine rumbled responsively into life. He shifted the automatic gear stick from P for Parked to D for Drive, while treading on the accelerator pedal. The jeep remained on the spot. Night Crawler stalked slowly toward the windscreen.

'Come on! *Come on!*' Nick was willing the jeep to move. 'I know I've done it right.'

Night Crawler stopped in front of them, peering inside as if unsure what to do. Before he could decide, Callie suddenly shouted, 'The handbrake!' Nick released it and the jeep lurched forward instantly. Night Crawler leapt out of the way at the last moment and the jeep stalled.

When Callie looked again, she could see Night Crawler speeding out through the villa's gateway and haring down the mud road.

'Well done,' she breathed. 'You've scared him away.' As Night Crawler receded into the distance, she added, 'I think we should go back inside.'

They locked the patio doors firmly behind them, and went upstairs together. They spent the rest of the night together in Callie's room with the light on.

When Callie came down for breakfast, her parents were sitting there as if nothing had happened. Callie couldn't believe her eyes. She hadn't heard the sound of them coming back in. 'How could you!' she demanded. 'How could you leave us on our own like that last night?'

Callie's mum looked up from the Greek yoghurt she was eating. She had olive-toned skin, pretty brown eyes and long, springy black hair, making her look like one of the locals. She was also fluent in Greek – both ancient and modern. 'What do you mean, Callie?'

'You weren't in your bedroom! We couldn't find you *anywhere*!'

'Well! What have you got to say for yourselves?' Nick had appeared at the bottom of the stairs.

There was a short tense silence.

'We were on the beach,' their dad said in the end. 'We were looking for loggerhead turtles.'

'Loggerhead turtles!' Callie pulled a disbelieving face.

'Yiannis said they sometimes come up on the beach at night to lay their eggs.'

Yiannis was the villa's Greek gardener, who was supposed to work three mornings a week but only seemed to turn up when he felt like it.

Callie frowned. There was barely any sand at Limani. It was mostly black rock with deep holes in it, as if someone had poured concrete unevenly all over the place. Not very inviting to creatures which laid their eggs in sand.

'Well, while you were out playing with turtles, we had an intruder,' she told them.

16

Callie's dad jumped up. 'What?'

'That's right! Someone was trying to get in and murder us in our beds,' added Nick dramatically.

Callie watched as the colour drained out of her mum's face. 'He was going round the villa trying to get in,' she said, sticking to the facts.

'Oh, darling!' Her mum embraced her in one arm and held out the other for Nick.

Their dad was looking just as concerned. 'What did he look like?'

'Greek!' said Callie, screwing up her face.

'So what happened?' Dad wanted to know.

'We tried ringing the police but we didn't know the number,' Callie said.

'One hundred,' her dad murmured automatically.

'Then we tried to run him over in the jeep,' said Nick excitedly.

Callie's dad cast an anxious glance through the patio doors. The rented jeep was a few metres away from where he'd parked it the day before, but was otherwise unharmed.

'We didn't know what else to do,' explained Callie, 'so we tried to get away.' She braced herself for the lecture about starting the jeep on their own but her dad seemed to be biting his tongue.

'It's not your fault,' said Callie's mum reasonably. 'We shouldn't have gone off without telling you...And we won't do it again!' she promised, staring at her husband.

He nodded, and walked out of the room. Callie

watched him go. Her parents were hiding something from her, there was no doubt about that. What were they really up to last night?

Callie wasn't going to let the mystery of where her parents had been spoil her day. She had plans of her own. She was going to find where King Akanon's Treasury was located. The Archaeological Museum in Thelta Town had one of the four clay tablets from King Akanon's triangular map on display. It was the only piece ever excavated! She knew this for a fact because it was *her* parents who had excavated it.

The lift into Thelta Town she'd been hoping for from her dad never materialised. He was catching up on sleep in a sun lounger by the side of the swimming pool. Mum had gone *back* to bed – as if she'd ever been there in the first place.

Callie packed sun cream, mineral water and some fruit into her pink backpack and checked how much money she had. A little over nine euros – around six pounds. It would have to be enough.

Nick was channel surfing on the TV as she went through the lounge. He'd spent hours since they'd arrived trying to find something recognisably English to watch.

'Where are you going?' he wanted to know.

'Out.'

'Do Mum and Dad know?'

'Not how the Latham family operates, is it?' replied Callie sarcastically.

'Right. I'm going out as well. I'm going to find those turtles.'

Callie sighed inwardly. She hated having to take responsibility for Nick. It shouldn't be her job. 'Ask Dad if you can go, and take your mobile with you.'

'Good idea! Then I can get some video of the turtles.'

Callie left him searching for a net to catch turtles in. He'd be lucky to find a net *or* turtles, she thought.

Villa Limani looked a lot less sinister without a stranger creeping round it: crisp and bright pastel green walls under a neat, red-tile roof. It was all part of a picturesque Theltan scene of white-painted villas and occasionally, a pastel shade of peach or rose pink. Under a perfect blue sky, the villas were scattered haphazardly down an ochre-coloured hillside dotted with brown scrub, green vineyards and dark olive groves. A yellow mud road led down to the beach. From the beach she could follow the shoreline all the way to Thelta Town, less than two kilometres to the north.

The road was bordered by rough walls. Patches of wild oregano was growing in the fields, smelling maddeningly of pizza because it was the herb they used and all Callie had in her backpack was fruit! Within a hundred metres the road came to an end with two massive boulders set up as a barrier. The vegetation changed abruptly too and herbs and shrubs were replaced by large cactuses, tall enough to pass as trees in England. The leaves resembled giant prickly tongues.

Callie had walked past the cactuses several times before

but had never seen sandalled feet sticking out from the bottom of one. Someone – a man – was hiding. She stopped. Maybe it was the night crawler, lying in wait for her. Then reason took over: Night Crawler had no idea she'd be walking down to the beach this morning.

'*Kalimera.*' Callie took a chance and called out the Greek word for good morning.

She stared right at the cactus, giving whoever was standing behind it little option but to step out from their hiding place.

'*Kalimera.*'

He couldn't have been much more than twenty years old, dark and unshaven and also very gawky with a disarming shyness about him – it wasn't the face she'd seen in front of the jeep last night. Apart from the sandals, he was dressed in a pair of baggy shorts and a grubby white vest. Callie knew him as Yiannis, the gardener who tended their villa's plants (when he could be bothered).

There was a beach towel lying in the shade of the cactus. Callie guessed Yiannis had been sunning himself when he was supposed to be working in their garden. He must have tried to hide when he heard her coming. No wonder he was looking so guilty.

'You are go for a swim?' he asked, his English not brilliant, but miles better than her Greek.

Callie shook her head. 'I'm walking to Thelta Town.'

'Shopping?'

'Museum.'

Yiannis raised an eyebrow at that. Obviously not his idea of fun. 'Have a nice day.'

Callie gave the word for thank you, '*Efharisto*,' and started to go. She turned back at the last minute. 'Yiannis? Are there any turtles on the beach here?'

'No. Not here,' said Yiannis without hesitation. 'A few, sometimes, at south of island.'

Villa Limani was definitely *not* on the south of the island. It was on the north-west coast.

Callie smiled at the gardener and left him to his bunking off. Dad hadn't been telling the truth about the turtles. What *had* her parents been up to last night?

Thelta Town was built along the waterfront, right at the northerly tip of the triangular island. The white bell tower of the church nestled between the fresh fish stalls and the colourful fruit and vegetable market.

Dozens of tavernas and café bars with seats outside crowded the harbour wall, where multi-coloured fishing boats, expensive yachts, cabin cruisers and a car ferry made the sea resemble rush hour in the centre of London.

Thelta Town's Archaeological Museum was hidden in a maze of streets behind the main shopping *palatia* in a small and unassuming concrete building painted white. It was open and only three euros to go in.

Two Greek policemen, wearing grey trousers and blue shirts, were examining the museum's doors as Callie walked inside.

'Where were you when I needed you?' she mumbled

under her breath, thinking about the intruder they'd had last night.

The museum had only four rooms, each dealing with an important period of Theltan history. The first had displays of prehistoric finds, flint tools and weapons, and black and white maps showing where they'd been found. The second room dealt with the Roman era on Thelta. There were Roman jars and pottery, coins and jewellery on show. There was an almost complete mosaic of Zeus, king of all the ancient gods, sending out lightning bolts from his fingers. In the third room was a representation of Thelta in the twentieth century. Cases of medals awarded in the First and Second World Wars stood beside mannequins dressed in Greek national costume. There were photographs taken immediately after earthquakes in 1930, 1954, and most recently in 1983, showing collapsed buildings and wide cracks in the roads.

But the final room was the one Callie was really interested in: the Mycenaean era of Thelta. And it was the best.

There was only one other person in the Mycenaean section. He was wiry and agile-looking, wearing a grubby white suit which was at least one size too big for him. As Callie walked past, he stared straight into her face, but only one eye followed her. The other remained motionless in its socket. It was made of glass. Callie hurried on.

The Mycenaean collection included: a bronze helmet, a dagger, and some small items of jewellery – trinkets really. Clearly these were not from King Akanon's

22

Treasury. There were a series of clay figurines, each a metre high and depicting different Greek gods. There was Poseidon, god of the sea and earthquakes, Aphrodite, goddess of beauty, and of course Zeus, king of all the gods. They were easy to recognise – her parents had excavated half of them, and copies of some of them were in their house!

Callie found herself gaping at a fresco taking up an entire wall. It was a mythological scene which had been painted onto drying plaster with plant dyes and minerals over three thousand years ago. Against a vivid, blood-red background was the image of a monster with the muscular body of a man and the head of a lion – jaws stretched wide in a killing attack. Three warriors lay broken and bleeding at the monster's feet, a fourth was still impaled upon its bloody sword.

'Magnificent, is it not? It was excavated not far from here. Only two kilometres down the coast.' The lady museum attendant had noticed that Callie was transfixed by the fresco. She was short and rounded with a sunny and open face framed by coppery bronze hair.

She must have guessed Callie's nationality, for she went on in English. 'It is from King Akanon's royal palace.'

'Yes, I know,' admitted Callie. The fresco was in one of the books her parents had written: full size it was staggering. 'It's called *The Capture of the Leonotaur* and was excavated fourteen years ago, by the English archaeologists Dan and Jill Latham.'

The museum attendant's mouth was open. Callie tried

not to laugh. 'Dan and Jill Latham are my parents,' she explained. 'They've been on about this picture since I was about one... They found the first clay tablet from King Akanon's map. In fact they were the ones who worked out that it was a corner of a map and there had to be three more pieces. They've been digging for the rest ever since.'

Callie suddenly became aware of Glass Eye, standing right behind her. He was listening to every word she said. She moved further around the room until the museum attendant was between her and Glass Eye.

She looked around. Something was missing, something vitally important. 'Where is it? The section of the map they found?'

The museum attendant's face fell. 'Had you visited yesterday I would have been able to show you, but last night the museum was broken into, and our famous map piece was stolen.'

Callie felt shocked. No wonder the police were outside checking the doors. Her parents were going to be incensed. 'Why would anyone want one segment of a four piece map?' she asked.

'Wealthy collectors will pay for *any* Mycenaean artefacts,' the museum attendant confided darkly. 'Now only one person will look upon King Akanon's clay tablet, where for the last fourteen years it has been on show to all.'

Callie felt like putting a comforting arm around the museum attendant, but gave her a bracing smile instead.

*

24

She was vaguely aware of Glass Eye talking to the two policemen as she left. She was on her way down the museum steps when he came running after her.

'Mees Latham, wait please.'

She paused on the last step. Glass Eye held his wallet open importantly to show her his identity card. It was a very police-like gesture. That explained his interest in what she'd been saying to the museum attendant. Her gaze lighted briefly on his dazzlingly blue eyes – one of them real, one of them not.

'Is this about the stolen clay tablet?' she asked.

'That is so,' Glass Eye nodded, tucking his wallet back inside his jacket. Callie thought she glimpsed a pistol strapped under his armpit. 'I must speak with you at police headquarters.'

Callie was taken aback. 'You want me to come *with* you?' What possible help could she be? If he wanted a description of the clay tablet, he should talk to the museum attendant.

'My car, it is this way.'

Hesitantly, Callie followed him.

There was a police car, white with a navy blue stripe down the side, parked in front of the museum. Glass Eye led her past it to a brown saloon instead.

Callie paused, alarm bells going off inside her head. What proof did she have that this man really was a policeman? He could have just been asking the police inside what time it was, and for all she knew, he'd just flashed his *Blockbuster Video* card at her.

'I think it's my parents you need to talk to,' she began. 'They're staying at the Villa Limani in Limani village...Ow!' Glass Eye had taken a tight grip of her arm and was steering her toward the brown car. The smell from his sweaty armpits was vile.

'We telephone parents from police station,' he growled. 'Now get in car.'

Callie knew this couldn't be right. She started to shout: 'Let go of me!'

In reply, Glass Eye yanked open the car door and started forcing her into the back.

Callie prayed he wasn't a real policeman, because of what she was going to do. She flicked her leg up behind her and felt the heel of her trainer make sharp contact with his shin. She twisted out of his grip and started running back towards the museum.

3
NIGHT CRAWLER RETURNS

Callie ran headlong into the two real policemen as they were coming out of the museum doors.

'*Voithia! Voithia!* Help! Help!' she blurted, as they gathered her up in their arms. She looked anxiously over her shoulder. Glass Eye had disappeared, and so had the brown saloon...

Callie lay awake that night, unable to sleep. It had been a pants day, and her visit to the Archaeological Museum had been a complete waste of time. Someone had stolen the very thing she had gone to look at.

She'd expected her parents to hit the roof when she told them about the missing clay tablet, but they hadn't seemed interested at all. 'You shouldn't have gone off on your own, Callie,' her mum had lectured her. 'I'm surprised at you!' Her dad barely looked up from a tray of pottery fragments.

Callie decided not to mention Glass Eye. That really would make them mad about her going off on her own. Then, at barely 10 o'clock, Mum and Dad announced it was time everyone went to bed. Holiday! It was more like a school night.

It was almost an hour later, and Callie still lay awake thinking about Glass Eye. Who was he really? Why had he tried to kidnap *her*? It was obviously something to do with King Akanon's map.

Then there was the thief. What kind of thief would ignore items of Mycenaean jewellery to steal just one segment of a four part map. One piece was useless on it's own. The museum attendant had said collectors would pay for *any* Mycenaean artefacts, so why had he ignored the jewellery and weapons?

Callie suddenly sat up in bed. Der! Whoever had stolen the clay tablet must have the other three pieces as well! That could be the only reason. Why bother with a few trinkets when you had the entire map to King Akanon's Treasury?

She settled down again but now she couldn't sleep because she was so excited. King Akanon's Treasury was about to be opened for the first time in over 3000 years.

'I wonder where it is?' she mused.

Callie tried closing her eyes. She opened them again immediately. What was that?

There was no window in her bedroom. Instead there was a glass door which opened out onto a small balcony. Light was shining through the balcony door; not speckled moonlight, but a brighter, more focused beam playing onto her bedroom wall. Then as suddenly as it had appeared it was gone.

A second later it came again, only this time it was three flashes and then nothing.

Callie climbed out of bed and opened the balcony door wide. The intense sound of screeching crickets ascended.

The beam came again: another three brief flashes – just

enough for Callie to locate the source. A small craft, perhaps a fishing boat, was in the shallows of the bay, signalling with a powerful torch.

There were so many villas perched against the hillside, the boat could be signalling to any one of them, yet Callie was convinced the signal was meant for Villa Limani.

Pausing only to change into a T-shirt and a pair of shorts, she hurried out of her bedroom and started to tiptoe barefoot down the staircase.

There was no sound from her parents' bedroom above. Maybe they were asleep. *Maybe* they'd gone off somewhere again!

Callie's heart quickened, as she slipped on her flip-flops and stepped out into the warm night air. She must be mad! Night Crawler could be around again, and what about the creature they'd heard roaring the evening before? She took a deep breath and headed through the iron gate, down the same mud road she'd taken that morning.

She didn't get far before she heard somebody chasing her down.

She spun around, stiffening her body against attack.

'Wait for me!'

'Nick!' Callie almost fainted.

Not only was he fully dressed, he was carrying a bulging backpack which looked as if it contained everything he had brought on holiday with him, and then some. He'd obviously been planning this all night.

'Go back,' she ordered.

'No, I'm coming with you.'

'You don't even know where I'm going.'

'You're following Mum and Dad.'

'No, I'm not.'

Nick looked surprised. Callie wasn't in the habit of lying to him. 'Where *are* you going then?'

Callie told him about the signalling she'd just seen from her bedroom.

'I'm definitely coming then,' decided Nick. 'You might need someone to save you if you get into trouble.'

'It's usually the other way round, Nick.' Callie groaned, but she gave in anyway. The fishing boat was probably long gone by now.

She was quite wrong. It hadn't gone at all. It was bobbing gently alongside a small jetty and the boatman was waiting on the beach. Callie motioned Nick behind one of the monstrous-looking cactuses sticking out of the ground.

The boatman seemed agitated, pacing the beach and intermittently looking at his wristwatch.

'What's he doing?' whispered Nick.

'Waiting for someone?' Callie hissed back, in a tone that said she thought it was obvious. Then the man turned, and moonlight suddenly caught his face.

Callie let out a little gasp. 'It's Night Crawler!' The man they'd nearly run over last night was back.

She searched for an explanation. Was he signalling to their villa because he thought someone else was staying there this month? Had he been expecting to meet them last night?

Nick was gripping her arm. A moment later, she realised why. Somebody tall was striding confidently down the path towards the beach.

'DAD!'

It was Nick this time who had made the exclamation. Both of them held their breath in case his voice had carried. There was no check in their dad's stride, and there was no doubt he was here to meet Night Crawler!

They didn't seem exactly pleased to see each other.

'What the hell were you playing at last night?' their dad demanded. 'You scared the living daylights out of my kids.'

'They scare *hell* out of me!' came the Greek-accented reply. 'The mobile phone number you give not work. How I know you not here last night?'

'Why should I have been? Everything was arranged for tonight,' came Dad's reply.

'I was ready one night early – I thought you in hurry.'

Dad and Night Crawler stood bristling at each other for a moment and then Dad relented. 'Well, it doesn't matter now.'

'Yes – misunderstanding . . . Shall we to business?'

There was perhaps only one thing which could have shocked Callie more. She saw it clearly in the moonlight – and it almost made her cry out. It was what Dad had come for. Night Crawler was handing over a triangular clay tablet with little sections cut out of it as if it fitted into a larger triangle. Callie recognised it instantly from all the books on Theltan archaeology. It was the piece of King

Akanon's map that had been stolen from the Archaeological Museum last night. Night Crawler was the man who had robbed the museum!

Dad was counting out money. Callie couldn't see whether the notes were tens, twenties, or fifties, but whatever denomination they were, the clay tablet was costing him a massive amount of money. The exchange was made and then her dad was striding back towards the villa with the clay tablet gripped tightly in his hand, while Night Crawler returned to his boat. Callie and Nick ducked out of sight.

'What was that all about?' spluttered Nick, when it was safe to speak.

'It's something to do with Dad's work,' said Callie. 'An artefact – and he probably doesn't want any other archaeologists knowing he's got it.' Or the police, she thought to herself.

'I can't wait to tell him we saw everything,' grinned Nick.

Callie shook her head. 'We can't say anything, Nick! Dad'll be furious if he finds out we were here spying on him.' She wasn't just afraid her dad would be angry. She was afraid they'd seen him receiving stolen goods.

'He'll probably think we're really clever for catching him out,' persisted Nick.

Callie could *really* see that happening. She tried a different approach. She shrugged her shoulders. 'Well, if you don't mind taking the risk.'

Nick frowned. 'What risk?'

'That Dad won't be really annoyed and change his mind about taking us dolphin-spotting this week, or snorkelling, or to the cave he said he would.'

Nick looked like he was having second thoughts. 'Who cares about his archaeology anyway?'

Callie's bedroom was right beneath her parents' room. Outside, the balconies jutted out from the bedrooms like open drawers in a desk. On sneaking back in, Callie found she'd left her balcony door open. Her parents must have done the same, because she could hear their voices – not raised, but certainly arguing, coming from above her.

'*Well?* Did you get it?' Callie's mum sounded like she hoped the answer was going to be 'No.'

'Yes, it's here.'

'Now we're in trouble with the Greek police.'

Callie was barely breathing. It *was* the museum's piece of the map!

'*We* didn't steal it,' Dad countered.

'You might find that hard to prove if Petros disappears.'

Petros, thought Callie. So that was Night Crawler's real name.

'There's nothing to connect us with him,' her dad was saying. 'Besides, the police are hardly going to be suspicious of *us* – we donated the piece to the museum in the first place.'

'If you're wrong, Dan, our careers are finished. No one would ever employ us again. We'd be ruined.'

'Jill, we *are* ruined. The bank's going to take away our

house and everything in it to pay off our debts, and even then it'll only clear a fraction of what we owe...'

Callie realised her mouth had dropped open. Mum and Dad were broke.

'And I've just spent the last of the cash on this!'

Callie could imagine her dad holding up the clay tablet.

'You haven't used what's in the piggy bank, have you?' said Mum anxiously.

'Of course not. That's for dire emergencies.' Her dad's voice was reassuring.

What piggy bank? thought Callie.

There was a pause and then her dad went on. 'It was your idea to fund our work on Thelta ourselves, when the museum wouldn't back us. If we don't succeed now it will cost us everything, and it's not just our future – it's the kids' too.'

Callie wanted to speak out. What kind of future would she and Nick have if their parents ended up in jail?

'This is awful, Dan, absolutely awful.'

'Look, we're not going to open King Akanon's Treasury and empty it. All we need is a few choice pieces to get us out of this hole.'

Everything had gone quiet and Callie was wondering if her parents had closed their balcony door, when her mum said, 'I want to see it – the complete map.'

Callie heard her parents' balcony door being closed.

They *have* got the whole map! she thought, closing her own door. She wondered how they'd collected the other three pieces, and if they'd taken risks like this before. Maybe the authorities already knew about the Latham family, and even now were closing in on them. She'd like to know how many more risks Dad would take in order to find and steal from King Akanon's Treasury? Callie wondered what was going to happen to them all, but most of all she wondered how she could get a look at that map!

4
GEORGIOU SKATELIOS

Callie was sitting under a beach umbrella replaying the events of last night in her head. Her parents were broke and they were going to steal from a Mycenaean king's treasury. Great!

This morning they had driven along the coast to the beach resort of Skuros, where they could snorkel off the beach and see the colourful, striped fish which came right to the water's edge. It was as if her mum and dad were trying to make up for disappearing the night before last, and then sleeping all day yesterday. They were acting like this was a normal holiday!

Callie found herself staring at the sea remembering last year...

...she was going to drown.

The grip of the water was dragging her ever downward. She was thrashing and flailing her arms, trying to kick for the surface with her legs. She felt as if she were in a water flume at an adventure park, but at the end of this ride she wouldn't find herself launched out into a heated swimming pool, she'd be dead.

Callie had no strength left. Any second now water would burst into her lungs and it would all be over.

Something new was gripping her. Something completely

different from the grip of the water. Vaguely, Callie was aware of a face beside her. It was her dad, and he was locking a strong arm around her... It wasn't enough! The current was too strong for him. Dad was going to drown with her. No sooner had Callie thought this than her mum was there with them. Together, her parents were fighting the sea for her and they were winning.

Callie's head broke the surface of the water and sweet, warm air rushed into her lungs. The suction from beneath released her and she was swimming freely – barely, but swimming nevertheless. Her mum and dad were swimming beside her.

She had almost drowned, caught in a lethal undercurrent. It had been a year ago and she would NEVER set foot in water again...

Her mum was coming back towards the beach umbrella – not from the sea, where Nick and Dad were snorkelling, but from a blue telephone kiosk outside a souvenir shop.

After a few pointless comments about the weather (of course it was hot! It was Greece in the summer!) she said, 'Callie, I want you to do something for me.'

Callie didn't answer. 'Darling...?'

'What?'

'Did you hear me?'

'You want me to do something for you,' said Callie. As long as it doesn't involve breaking into a museum, she thought sourly.

'I want you to be on my side.'

Callie looked surprised. What was that supposed to mean?

'The thing is,' her mum went on, 'Dad and I have got to work.'

'I don't mind,' said Callie, 'You're always working when we're on holiday. We can help.'

'It's a bit more complicated than that.'

You can say that again, thought Callie.

'We're going to need to work on our own this time.'

Callie didn't even bother to ask why – she knew perfectly well. 'Where's all this leading?' she asked instead.

'We want you to spend the rest of the summer with Aunt Callista.'

'No way!' said Callie, without having to think about it. The rest of the summer with boring Aunt Callista, in her tiny flat full of mangy cats that smelt of wee. So that's who she'd been calling from the kiosk.

'This is all because of Dad buying stolen clay tablets, isn't it?'

Her mum put her hand to her mouth in shock. 'How do you…?'

'I saw him! *And* Petros – last night. And then you forgot your balcony door was open so I heard everything. Absolutely *everything*.'

Her mum looked like she was going to throw up. Finally she said, 'Okay… If you heard, you understand why I want you and Nick to go back to England.'

Callie understood all right. Her parents were criminals.

'You'll be safe with Aunt Callista,' her mum rationalised.

'Isn't it your job to keep us safe?' retorted Callie, and then immediately regretted it when she saw how hurt her mum looked. To avoid saying anything worse she got up and said, 'I'm going to go and buy some postcards. Doesn't look like I've got much more holiday left to send them in, does it?'

The souvenir shop had inflatable turtles hanging outside, along with day-glo lilos and beach balls. There were snorkels, masks and flippers, beach towels with maps of Thelta on them, and at least three racks of postcards.

They were also selling souvenir King Akanon's maps in red clay. One section had been copied from the museum's clay tablet, with the other three pieces obviously a complete guess. Along the bottom of the triangle it said: GREETINGS FROM THELTA. Probably *not* on the original, thought Callie.

She began choosing postcards at random. Her mind was a confusion of garbled thoughts. She couldn't think of anything worse than being sent back to London. She wouldn't know what was happening to her parents. She wouldn't know if they were in trouble or even if they'd found King Akanon's treasure. She would spend every minute until she saw them again worrying herself sick, and babysitting Nick, while being attacked by smelly cats!

How could they do this! How could they do this to *her*!

'Two euros, please.'

Callie realised she had wandered inside the souvenir shop and handed over several postcards to the woman behind the counter. She paid with two one-euro coins.

The shop assistant put the postcards into a paper bag and added a free pen to write them with.

Callie smiled. 'Thank you. *Efharisto.*' As she turned to go, she noticed some newspapers on a counter, and wondered if there was anything about the museum robbery.

Callie stopped dead in horror. Not only was there something about the museum robbery, there was a picture of Night Crawler on the front of every newspaper! Callie stared at the headlines without comprehension. She turned back to the shop assistant.

'Can you tell me what this says?' she asked, pointing at one of the newspapers.

The shop assistant looked blankly at her.

Callie underlined the headline on the newspaper with her finger. 'Erm, this says?'

The shop assistant struggled. 'Erm, Man...Murder.' She shrugged her head sadly. 'Not worry. Murder not much on Thelta.'

Callie was already running from the shop, her mind racing. Why had 'Petros' been murdered? Was it for the money her dad had paid him, or was it something to do with King Akanon's map? Callie felt a pang of grief. She had seen him only the night before and now he was dead. She felt a shiver. She must have been one of the last people to see him alive.

She froze, causing two garishly-dressed tourists to almost fall over her. What if the police thought her dad had killed Petros to keep him quiet? What if she had to provide Dad with an alibi? She'd seen him go straight back to the villa and then heard him arguing with her mum. Mum could prove that he hadn't gone out again.

Then she thought of something else. If Petros had been killed, there was no one to say what had happened to the clay tablet. Dad was safe! Callie wanted to cheer. Instead she just smiled broadly and ran back across the road to their beach umbrella.

Her mum wasn't pleased at all – she was horrified. Now she was even more adamant about sending them both back to England. First though, she charged off to buy the newspaper.

That was it. The holiday, and any adventure with it, was over.

Dinner that evening was like the first day of a new school term – nobody wanted to be there.

Dad had driven to their favourite taverna, *Ta Stafilia*, The Grapes, to break the news to Nick that he and Callie were being sent home early, while Mum and Dad stayed on to work.

'*I'm* not going back, so forget it,' was Nick's typically hot-headed response.

'That's not how it works, Nick,' said his dad, equally determined.

'You can't make me,' raged Nick.

'Er, I think I can.' Dad and Nick were as stubborn as each other.

They were sitting on *Ta Stafilia's* long balcony, under a trellis festooned with ripening grapes. The taverna was set so close to the lapping sea that they could feed the fish by throwing little pieces of bread into the water.

'Why can't we stay and help? That's what we usually do?' Nick demanded.

Their mum intervened. 'The best way to help us, Nick, is to do what we ask without making a fuss.'

'Why aren't *you* saying anything?' Nick shot at Callie.

'Waste of breath,' Callie told him.

'Is this all because of that archaeology thing you bought last night?' Nick said loudly. 'The thing you don't think we know about?' He obviously felt freed of any restrictions on mentioning last night now that they were going home anyway.

Callie's dad almost choked on his pork. He cast anxious glances towards the other tables to see if anyone was listening, then lowered his voice: 'One more word, Nick, and it's not just the end of this holiday. It's the end of all holidays – ever.'

Nick's face stiffened somewhere between anger and tears. 'Fine by me!'

He flung his chair back and stamped down the balcony steps, leaving his burger and chips untouched – a first. Moments later they could see him on the beach unsuccessfully trying to hit the fish with rocks.

'Callie, try and make your brother understand,' Mum began, but Callie was pushing back her own chair.

'Why don't you do your own dirty work, Mum?'

Callie wandered down to the beach. It wasn't much bigger than the average garden at home, and instead of sand there were pebbles and rocks reaching right under the turquoise and sapphire sea.

She saw Manolis, the taverna owner's son, fishing off a flat boulder poking out from the beach into the sea. He was the same age as Callie and had learned very good English from all the tourists who came to The Grapes. Callie thought he was gorgeous; his dark, Mediterranean colouring somehow making him seem older. Callie and Nick had befriended him the first night they came here to eat, and they saw him each dawn and dusk in his little red and yellow boat, checking the lobster pots in the bay in front of their villa. Half the seafood eaten at the taverna was caught by Manolis.

'Your brother has found a new way of fishing,' he joked, as Callie joined him. Nick was still lobbing stones into the water.

'Don't worry, he can't hit anything,' Callie reassured him.

'You and Niko are not happy today,' said Manolis, using the Greek version of Nick's name. 'You don't like Thelta anymore?'

'That's the problem: we do, and now we have to go home.'

Manolis frowned. 'I thought you were here for the summer.' He reeled in his fishing line and placed the rod on the ground.

'Our parents have to work and we'll be in the way – apparently.'

'They dig up Thelta for history?'

'Mmm,' Callie nodded vaguely. She had noticed that Nick was talking to a stocky-looking man, who was pointing to a small boat with a little cabin and an outboard motor. It was painted blue and white, the same colours as the Greek flag, and was tied up at a stone jetty at the far end of the beach.

'Manolis, who's that talking to Nick?'

Manolis followed Callie's gaze and then shook his head. 'I don't know him.'

'Where are they going?'

Nick and the stranger were walking purposely towards the boat. Nick was laughing and smiling.

'Come on!' said Callie and started to run. Manolis snatched up his fishing rod and chased after her.

Callie gave a fleeting look at the balcony of the taverna. Her parents were in serious conversation and had seen nothing wrong. She shouted up to them as she sprinted underneath, 'Mum! Dad!' but they didn't hear, and stopping to make them hear would lose valuable time.

The man had reached his boat and was helping Nick aboard.

'Hurry,' yelled Manolis, overtaking her, 'or it'll be too late.'

Callie could see for herself he was right. She scampered after him, trying to negotiate the rocks at speed.

The man was still on the jetty, untying the mooring rope as first Manolis, and then Callie came charging up to him. He was wearing shorts and a vest, and though he was only medium height, his muscular arms looked as if he spent hours working out in a gym. He had a tattoo of a roaring lion's head on his massive shoulder.

Callie ignored him, and spoke directly to Nick. 'Get off that boat, Nick.'

Nick looked ashamed at being ordered about by an older sister. 'No. I'm going with Lion Tattoo. We're off to see Loggerhead turtles.'

'Lion Tattoo' beamed at Callie, still holding the end of the mooring rope. 'You come too, yes? See turtles.'

Callie noticed that his smile did not extend to his eyes, which were cold and calculating.

'Nick, the turtles nest on the south coast of the island. They don't come up this far.'

'But Dad said—'

'Dad was wrong,' said Callie firmly. She looked at Manolis to back her up.

Manolis shook his head emphatically. 'The turtles don't come here, Niko.'

Nick pointed at Lion Tattoo. 'But he knows where they are. He's seen them.'

Lion Tattoo gave up on Callie, and jumped into the boat, making it sway in the water. He went to the outboard motor, and yanked the starter cord. The outboard spluttered into life with a puff of petrol smoke. The propeller spun and he began to lower it into the water, his false smile completely gone.

'Off that boat NOW!' shouted Callie.

Nick looked unsure for a moment; even he must have

seen that Lion Tattoo wasn't looking so friendly anymore. 'Okay.' He scrambled to the edge of the boat nearest the jetty.

THWACK! Lion Tattoo swung an oar right at Nick's head. He missed him by inches, the blade slicing a splinter of wood off the side of the boat.

'JUMP!' yelled Callie, but Lion Tattoo was lifting the oar to swing again, and this time he couldn't miss.

There was a scream of agony. It took Callie a moment to realise that it wasn't from Nick. Lion Tattoo had dropped the oar and was scratching dementedly at his shoulder – the barbs of a fish-hook were biting deeply into his flesh. Blood was seeping from the tattooed lion's jaws. Manolis had hooked both lion and man with his rod.

Nick leapt for the jetty and clung onto it, his legs dangling. Callie hauled him to safety by the scruff of his neck.

Manolis cut away the fishing line and his 'catch' with a penknife. Lion Tattoo hesitated threateningly for a moment and then started steering his boat across the water, hurling angry Greek insults at all three of them. Manolis refused to translate.

As they walked under the balcony, Callie's mum and dad still hadn't noticed that anything was wrong.

'What was that about?' asked Manolis, as they reached his fishing spot on the flat rock.

'I don't know.' Callie wondered if it didn't have something to do with King Akanon's Treasury.

46

Unimaginable riches were at stake. It looked like her parents were right: she and Nick *would* be safer back in England. All of them would be safer back in England!

'Manolis?' she asked. 'Do people ever get kidnapped on Thelta?'

Manolis frowned, so Callie tried to explain *kidnapped*, 'Taken and then only given back to their family if they pay a lot of money.'

Manolis nodded. 'It has happened, but it is not very common. Rich men's children, they are usually protected by bodyguards.' Manolis mimed flexing his muscles – somebody strong.

'I've got something better than a bodyguard,' said Nick. 'I've got an older sister and Manolis, with his fishing rod of vengeance.' It was the first time Nick had spoken since his escape, and he seemed to have cheered right up. He was obviously excited at cheating a would-be kidnapper. He'd have a great time telling his sidekicks at school about his brush from an oar-wielding maniac.

They sat down on the flat rock, with their feet dangling into the cool water.

A gold-coloured Mercedes Benz, stylish and expensive, was pulling up alongside The Grapes. Instantly Manolis's parents came running down the steps to greet the man climbing out of the driver's seat.

'Who's that? The King of Thelta?' said Nick.

Callie shot her brother an admonitory look. Manolis's parents greeted their own mum and dad as if they were Prince Charles and Camilla. They were only making a tiny bit more of a fuss over Mr Mercedes.

He was maybe as old as sixty, with a full head of white hair, greased back from his forehead with precision. He wore a smart, perfectly-tailored, cream-coloured suit.

'His name is Georgiou Skatelios,' Manolis told them. 'He is a kind of king, with his own kingdom: Skatelios Island.'

'The island in the bay!' exclaimed Callie. She suddenly remembered the roaring cries they'd heard from Skatelios Island. 'Manolis, does he keep a lion on that island?'

Manolis looked astonished. 'A lion?'

'Yeah! That's right – we heard one,' said Nick eagerly.

Manolis shook his head. 'I don't think so.'

After a pause Callie asked, 'How come he has his own island, anyway?'

'He was very poor. He had nothing until he earned enough money to buy a very small boat which he hired out to tourists. One day he had more boats and more tourists, and then many boats and many tourists. He was *plousios,* rich, by the time he was twenty years old.'

Nick looked as if he was working out how to buy *his* first boat.

'Now he has motorboats and a helicopter always standing by to bring him to Thelta or the mainland,' Manolis went on. 'He keeps his gold Mercedes on Thelta, to drive himself around the island, to meetings or parties or when he goes hunting with dogs.'

'Hunting with dogs?' Callie looked disgusted.

'He hunts rabbits on the plains along the south coast.'

'Have you ever been to Skatelios Island?' asked Nick.

Manolis laughed. 'No. Maybe he'll ask me when I become president of Greece...He may invite your parents though. He is a great collector of Mycenaean artefacts. He even has a private museum in his mansion.'

Callie shivered. This couldn't be a coincidence. Somehow Skatelios knew that her mum and dad had King Akanon's map – and if he'd found out from Petros, he could be his killer. And what was the betting that Lion Tattoo was working for him as well?

'Does he eat at your taverna often?' asked Callie.

Manolis was shaking his head. 'I don't remember him ever coming here before.' That settled it.

Manolis's parents were leading Skatelios to their best table, but Skatelios pointed to another one – one that was already occupied. It was right next to their mum and dad, and Skatelios was determined to sit there. The diners, already halfway through their meal, would have to move. Clearly this was a man who was not accustomed to being denied. As soon as he was seated, Skatelios angled his chair round to speak to their parents.

'I think we'd better go back to our table,' said Callie. She wanted to hear exactly what Mr Skatelios had to say.

'Have a safe journey home,' smiled Manolis.

'Thanks, Manolis...And thanks for saving Nick.'

When they reached their table, Callie slipped quietly back into her chair, and for once, Nick followed her example. Skatelios flashed them a look of resentment, as if they'd both defied him. Now Callie was certain Lion Tattoo had been ordered to kidnap Nick. No wonder

49

Skatelios looked mad. Because Lion Tattoo had failed, Skatelios was having to try something else.

'Maybe it's time you left Thelta, Mr Latham, Mrs Latham. We have many good local archaeologists.' His tone was friendly, though Callie thought what he was saying sounded a lot like a threat. He spoke English flawlessly with an American accent. Maybe he'd picked it up from wealthy American clients.

'We're not excavating at the moment, Mr Skatelios,' Callie's dad said. 'We're merely involved in research.'

'I've heard about this research, Mr Latham. There are four pieces of this research. Perhaps you should hand over the entire work to me and stay in *one* piece yourself.'

Nick was mouthing something to Callie. 'What's he on about?' Nick was the only one at the table who didn't understand.

'I have Mycenaean blood, Mr Latham,' boasted Skatelios. 'My DNA matches that of King Akanon's royal line.' Callie wondered if that was true. 'Who better to act as custodian of King Akanon's legacy?'

'I can't help you, Mr Skatelios. I have no more idea where King Akanon's Treasury is than you do.' Their dad stood up and left the money for the meal on the table. Everyone else stood up.

Skatelios ground his teeth at this obvious dismissal. It was clearly a very long time since anyone had defied him.

'Enjoy your holiday, Mr Latham, Mrs Latham,' he recovered his voice. 'Look after your children well. Thelta can be a very dangerous island.'

5
SHORTCUT DOWN
THE MOUNTAIN

Nick was talking excitedly about his 'Triumph over Lion Tattoo', as they climbed into the black jeep. 'He must have thought we were really rich to try and kidnap me.'

Callie's mum had turned white, and Dad was looking extremely worried.

'He practically *forced* me into his boat,' Nick went on, telling the story quite differently from the way Callie remembered it. 'But when Callie and Manolis turned up, I did this amazing, long jump from his boat to the jetty. It was brilliant.'

Nobody else looked as if they thought it was brilliant.

'I think I was really brave...' Nick looked at everyone's faces. 'What's wrong with everybody?'

When nobody answered, he went on, 'Well, now you know me and Callie can look after ourselves, can we stay?'

'NO!' both parents had answered at once.

Although Villa Limani wasn't far along the coast from The Grapes taverna, there was no direct route. The two places were linked by a road which headed first into the foothills of Mount Thelta, Thelta's only mountain, and then doubled back on itself like a wishbone.

The road was narrow and separated from a terror-drop into the sea by only a low, and not very reassuring-looking metal barrier. Every so often Callie's dad had to swerve to avoid fragments of rock that had rolled off the hillside and created obstacles on the worn tarmac.

As the jeep climbed the hill, the sun was setting over the sea like a crimson shield, and Mount Thelta glowed as if gilded in Greek gold.

KERLANG!

'What was that?' Callie twisted in her seat to stare up at the grey mountainside, thinking the jeep had been hit by a falling rock.

There was another bang, accompanied by a tooth-aching, grinding sound. This time it came from right beside Callie, and when she looked she could no longer see the mountain. A scarlet red truck was side by side with their jeep, steering them towards the steel barrier.

'He's trying to force us over!' Dad was fighting to keep the jeep on the road, while trying to accelerate away from the truck. Everyone else was transfixed by the barrier, which was inching closer and closer. If the barrier gave way, they would drop to the sea and rocks fully half a kilometre below!

There was a another loud BANG, and an ear-splitting SCREECH as the truck came into their side again.

The jeep lurched and glanced off the barrier at eighty kph. Callie's dad swore loudly and her mum screamed – something Callie had never heard her do before. Nick was breathing so fast in terror that he sounded like a panting dog.

Callie gaped out of the window on her side of the jeep and found herself staring straight into the eyes of the truck driver. He was leaning across his cab to look down into their jeep, and had fastened his startlingly blue stare right on her.

'It's Glass Eye,' murmured Callie.

'Who?' Callie's mum twisted round.

'He tried to kidnap me at the museum. He's got a glass eye.'

'Callie! Why didn't you tell us?'

Callie dropped her gaze, but only as far as Glass Eye's bare, wiry arm, and the tattoo of a lion's head on his scrawny bicep: Lion Tattoo number two! There was no doubt then – he worked with Lion Tattoo One. And who was the head of the pride? Skatelios. He had to be. Hadn't he said that Thelta could be a dangerous place?

'LOOK!' Their mum was pointing at the steel barrier a hundred metres ahead. There was an entire section missing! More than enough to send a jeep through.

'He's going to kill us!' screamed Nick. He was on the side nearest the barrier – the side nearest the fall.

'I'm going to try and lock the brakes!' shouted their dad. 'Get ready for it.'

Mum twisted round to look at Callie and Nick. 'Jam yourselves in. Put your feet up against the front seats. NOW!'

Callie and Nick reacted immediately.

'Ready?' It was Callie's dad.

'We're ready,' yelled Callie, for all of them.

Mum gripped the handbrake lever and shouted, 'DO IT!' She yanked on the handbrake at the precise moment that Callie's dad, almost standing up in his seat, threw all his weight onto the foot brake.

At any other time the jeep might have slewed into an irretrievable spin, but there was nowhere for it to swing, pinned solid as it was between the barrier and the truck. Instead it decelerated rapidly as brake-pad rubber gripped brake-disc metal. The jeep juddered. Steel could be heard buckling and tearing as the truck failed to slow and pitched ahead, careening in front of them.

Smoke spiralled from the truck's tyres as Glass Eye jammed on the brakes.

The two scarred and battered vehicles came to a complete stop barely twenty metres apart – the jeep just before the gap in the barrier, the truck just past it.

Callie's dad was ramming the gear stick into reverse to escape the way they had come. But Glass Eye seemed satisfied with his night's work. With a clash of gears and the roar of a powerful engine, he drove away, clattering down the hill.

'He's going,' gasped Nick unnecessarily.

We're no good to Skatelios dead, thought Callie. He'll never find King Akanon's Treasury without the clay tablets. *That* was just a warning.

They arrived back at the villa without further incident. Luckily the jeep had still been drivable even though it looked like it *had* crashed down a mountain, and the few other cars they'd passed had slowed down to look at them.

They were in the villa's lounge, where Callie's dad had gathered them to explain why someone had just smashed up their jeep. Most of it Callie already knew – about King Akanon hiding three great keys around the island, and then making a map of where precisely they had been hidden, and about Petros being murdered. Her interest piqued when he finally got to how he and Mum had collected the clay tablets one by one.

'The first piece we excavated fourteen years ago,' he said. 'Before either of you were born. It was our first dig on Thelta.'

'I wish we'd never set foot on this island,' contributed Callie's mum bitterly, pacing the room.

'The Theltan authorities called us in when building work uncovered some Mycenaean remains. That's when we unearthed the clay tablet which went to the Archaeological Museum.'

'Until you stole it back,' said Callie coldly.

Nick took a moment to catch on. 'You stole it from the museum!' His tone sounded as much impressed as shocked.

'No – the man you saw last night stole it from the museum.'

'Oh, *that's* fine then,' sneered Callie. 'As long as it wasn't you.'

Her dad ignored her. 'The second clay tablet was found buried along with a Mycenaean warrior in a tomb on Mount Thelta. That should have gone to the museum as well but the archaeologist kept it himself.'

'You again, I suppose!' snorted Callie.

'No – a colleague, and he kept it until he died last year. He left it to us in his will.'

Dad took a sip of water before carrying on. 'The third piece we found last year while diving a site on the east coast of Thelta.'

The thin, transparent curtain over the open patio door rustled, in a sudden warm breeze from the sea. Everyone started, and Nick even gave out a little cry. It was as if King Akanon's ghost had finally returned from Troy.

Callie's dad crossed to the patio door, pointed his car keys at the battered jeep to lock it, and then slid the door closed. The bolt slotted into place with a secure clunk.

'Where was I?'

'The fourth piece,' Callie prompted him.

'The internet,' Callie's mum took over the story.

Callie could scarcely find her voice. 'The internet? You don't mean – *eBay*?'

'Not quite, but similar. Someone calling themselves "Akanon", with a map piece to sell. I made a bid for it as a joke, and it turned out to be the real thing.'

'In the meantime we'd managed to translate a pottery inscription and worked out exactly where King Akanon's underground treasury was located,' said Callie's dad. 'Our original excavation had missed it by only metres... This week we found an antechamber and the stairs leading down to the Treasury doors.'

'But you said they were building on top of the original

excavation,' interrupted Callie with a frown. 'How did you . . . ?'

'We bought the building last year,' her dad said.

'Villa Limani!' exclaimed Callie. 'The strange noises that woke us up that night! It was you!' It suddenly all made sense. Villa Limani was built right on top of King Akanon's Treasury. No wonder she'd been dreaming!

'Wait a minute!' shouted Nick. 'YOU *OWN* THIS PLACE?' He screwed up his face in disbelief. 'I thought we were on HOLIDAY.'

'Why haven't *we* seen it?' interrupted Callie. 'How do you get *under* the villa?'

'It's not important any more, is it?' said Callie's mum, with a note of finality. 'That's the whole story! Because the madman who tried to have you both kidnapped, and force us over a cliff, can have the clay tablets. We're getting the next plane out of here.'

After a pause, Callie's dad nodded. It was the only thing they could do. It wasn't as if they could go to the police – not after he'd bought the stolen map piece.

'Come on. Let's all get some sleep,' sighed Mum softly, as if all the life had finally drained from her. Callie was still wondering: How on earth do they get under the villa?

Callie awoke bathed in sweat – disturbed for a third night in a row. She sat up in bed and listened intently, her lips slightly parted. She could hear crying.

She pulled on a top, some shorts and her trainers and opened her bedroom door. Tiptoeing across the landing, she knocked very quietly on the door opposite. The crying stopped abruptly.

Callie opened the door. In the remains of the moonlight, breaking through the balcony doors opposite, Nick was staring at her with a set expression.

'Are you okay?' she asked.

'*Yes!*'

'I heard you crying,' she said sympathetically.

'No, you didn't.'

'It's all right to be scared you know.'

'I'm not scared.'

'*I* am,' admitted Callie.

Nick frowned. 'Really?'

''Course I am, you muppet. We could have been killed tonight! I'm not stupid.'

'I wasn't crying,' insisted Nick.

Callie looked into his eyes, fighting with herself over allowing him to keep his pride by lying to her.

'I might have cried a bit,' he admitted.

Callie went and sat on his bed. 'Who do you think's worse – Glass Eye or Lion Tattoo?'

'Lion Tattoo. How did you get away from Glass Eye – before?'

'I kicked him in the shin and ran to two policemen.'

'Good one.' After a beat, Nick went on, 'I still don't want to go home.'

'You really are a muppet then, aren't you?' said Callie, then added, 'I don't want to either, and I'm not sure Mum and Dad do.'

'Then why can't we stay and find the treasure?'

'Er, let me think: SKATELIOS...And the fact he's MENTAL. Did you hear what he said to Dad? *I've got Mycenaean blood. I've got the same DNA.*'

'Maybe he has. Maybe he's checked.'

Callie screwed up her face. 'You mean he's taken DNA from ancient remains.'

'Yep – bodies. Manolis said he'd got his own private museum. Maybe he's got royal skeletons.'

Callie thought about it and nodded. 'I suppose a lot of Mycenaean tombs *have* been excavated over the years.'

Nick sighed again. 'And *we* didn't even get to see the map.'

Callie chewed her lip for a moment. 'Well, we can do something about that.'

Nick looked baffled. 'How?'

'I think I know where Dad will have hidden something that valuable.'

The cellar at Villa Limani was lit by a bare electric bulb hanging from the ceiling. There was an unpleasant smell of damp, paint was peeling off the white-washed walls – and one entire corner was covered with black furry mould.

Trays of pottery fragments were stacked on metal shelf units and in large crates, and there was a table with a magnifying stand for examining finds in detail. There was some geophysical equipment which Dad had borrowed from someone on the island. It could survey a dig site like an archaeologist's x-ray machine.

Callie glanced at a full-length mirror hanging down one of the walls, and spotted what she was looking for in the reflection – two Ancient Greek wine jars. She went over to the largest one and picked it up by the rim without ceremony. It was slender at the neck and base, and wide around the middle with a handle on each side.

'Careful!' warned Nick.

Callie examined the amphora. The narrow opening made it suitable for only oil or wine. She placed her fingers around the top rim and started to twist. 'I saw Dad do this once. He must have had it specially made.'

The amphora started to unscrew at the widest part, opening into two pieces.

Callie put the top down on the table and reached into the bottom. One by one, she drew out four clay tablets.

'Wow!' Nick breathed.

Callie felt her heart pounding powerfully in her chest. King Akanon himself had held these tablets, and now she was holding them!

There were three pieces shaped similarly: the outside edges forming the main triangle. The fourth piece was smaller, an equilateral triangle and it—

'That bit fits in the middle,' prompted Nick.

Callie cleared a space on the table and carefully assembled King Akanon's map. It formed a triangle within a triangle, around forty centimetres along each side, and a centimetre thick. The surface of the clay was covered with symbols, pictograms, ancient Greek writing and lines of measurement.

Now she could see why no one had ever deciphered the map using one single piece: distance was written on the centre piece, but direction was written on each corner piece. You had to have all four pieces.

'Where are they then?' demanded Nick. 'Where are the keys?'

Callie pulled a face. 'Is that a joke?'

'Don't you know?' Nick was flabbergasted.

'Of course I don't! It needs deciphering.'

Callie looked down at the map again. She had only wanted to *see* it, but now she wished more than anything she *could* interpret it as well.

She was reminded of the thing people said when they couldn't understand something: 'It's all Greek to me.'

CRASH!

It sounded like an explosion had blown out the patio doors in the room above them. Callie had ducked instinctively, and she could see Nick had too. They both now dared to look at the cellar ceiling, half afraid it was about to come crashing down on top of them.

'What was that?' Nick spluttered.

Callie didn't need to hear the shouting Greek voices to guess what was happening. 'Skatelios!'

6
ESCAPE WITH THE MAP

Callie piled up the pieces of the map.

'What are you doing?'

'We have to give them to him. That's what Mum and Dad decided. It's the only way he'll let us all go.' She started up the stone steps which led out of the cellar. 'Stay here...'

Callie opened the cellar door a little at a time. She didn't want to run straight into Lion Tattoo or Glass Eye. She would take her chances with their boss, but not with them.

She could see quite clearly from where she was. The dawn light was spilling through the villa's windows. On the other side of the cellar door was another short flight of stone steps – leading up to the lounge and kitchen. Through the gap at the top of the cellar door, Callie could see everything that was going on in the lounge – yet because the cellar was only a few centimetres above ground level, nobody could see her.

The lounge looked as if somebody had exploded a bomb. There were shards of glass covering the tiled floor. A bookcase was in splinters, its contents vomited over the room. A sofa was upturned and the dining table was tottering on three legs. The cause of all this mayhem and destruction was their jeep, parked in the middle of the room. One of Skatelios's men must have driven it right through the patio doors to get in.

Callie could hear her parents being dragged out of their room, two floors up. At least two men were shouting at them in Greek. Callie's parents were shouting back.

'You can have the map!' came her dad's voice.

'What have you done with my children?' shouted her mum. Then it sounded as if she was asking the same question in Greek.

Callie took a deep breath. She could make this nightmare end. All she had to do was hand over the clay tablets. She started to open the door further, just as two men walked into the lounge: Lion Tattoo and Glass Eye, the two men she was desperate to avoid. Skatelios didn't seem to be with them.

Glass Eye was handing Lion Tattoo a pistol. He said in English, 'Bang bang – no witnesses.' A gap-toothed smile broke out on Lion Tattoo's face. He wasn't going to argue.

Callie quietly pulled the door shut. Skatelios wasn't going to let them go! She tried to think. If she could escape with King Akanon's map, there was a chance she could trade it for their lives. Escape? She stared around the cellar in dismay. There was no way out. She retreated back down the steps.

'What's happening?' demanded Nick. 'You've still got the map.'

'I overheard them. As soon as they've got the map, they're going to kill us.'

She looked desperately for somewhere to hide. The

only place remotely possible was inside the crates. She ran over to one and started removing its contents: pieces of Mycenaean pottery packed in bubble-wrap.

Nick was rooted to the spot, staring mutely at her.

'Help me with the other crate,' Callie ordered.

Nick hesitated.

'Come on!'

Nick was finally stung into action and started emptying the second crate.

All the time, a voice was screaming inside Callie's head: THIS WILL NEVER WORK! Skatelios's men were certain to examine the crates in their search for the clay tablets. If Callie left them on the table for them to find, she would have nothing to bargain with. They were trapped. No – they were dead.

Nick suddenly screamed and stumbled backwards. A brown lizard was running up his bare arm. It must have been hiding in the crate. Callie shot forward and snatched the lizard off and threw it into a corner.

She was too late. Nick had fallen against one of the tall, metal shelf units and it was already crashing over. It smashed into the second shelf unit with such force that that too began to fall. They hit the mouldy cellar wall together with a deafening crash, and continued on through plaster and bricks.

'Sorry,' mumbled Nick.

Already they could hear shouting from the room above. Lion Tattoo and Glass Eye now knew exactly where they were. And Nick had just made a way out!

'Come on!' Callie climbed over the shelf units and through the hole in the wall. In the light penetrating through from the cellar, she could see the villa's generator, and the large heating-oil tank. It was the generator bunker. Above her was the hatch to the outside world.

Callie started trying to force open the hatch cover with the heels of her hands. Behind her she heard someone clambering over the wreckage in the cellar, and looked back to see Lion Tattoo's ugly face appear at the hole in the wall. He put his strength to good use, tearing apart the rest of the wall to get through.

Nick jumped to help Callie, and the hatch cover burst open with a clatter. They scrambled out into the early morning light.

There was no one on guard outside the villa, but as they ran for the gate, Glass Eye and a smartly dressed man came tearing out through what was left of the patio doors. Glass Eye pointed at them and shouted. Callie looked down at her hand. She was still carrying the four clay tablets, and he had seen them. There would be no let-up now. Skatelios's men couldn't go back to their boss empty-handed.

She dashed through the gate and past a green jeep and a brown saloon. She ran instinctively for the beach.

'You're going the wrong way!' yelled Nick. 'We've got to get to the village.'

'We can't outrun cars,' Callie shouted back. 'Downhill, we've got a chance of making it to where those boulders cut off the road.'

In the time it had taken to explain, Callie heard car engines being started, revved and then the squealing of tyres. She risked a look – the jeep and the saloon were only fifty metres back – coming on fast.

Lion Tattoo was at the wheel of the green jeep, and it sported deadly bull bars on the front. It could only be moments before those bars would slam into them, and drag them under the heavy tyres.

Callie ran as hard as she'd ever run. She could see the boulders ahead.

'Come on!' screamed Nick, surging ahead. 'Come on, Callie.'

The roar of the jeep's engine was so loud behind her, Callie knew she was seconds from being mowed down. Then she was leaping over the first boulder, and the engine roar became a skidding noise instead, as Lion Tattoo slammed on the brakes.

Callie kept running. She was gasping for air, but Lion Tattoo and Glass Eye jumped out of their vehicles and started chasing them down on foot. She had to keep going!

Three shots rang out within a second. Callie heard flesh exploding beside her and was splattered with a sticky juice. It took her a moment to realise that the bullets had ripped into one of the giant cactuses.

'Callie!'

'Keep going! I'm all right.'

Callie raced onto the rock beach. Every so often there was a water-filled hole, some half a metre deep, which took skill to miss at speed, but Callie and Nick were experts at dodging them after spending hours exploring the beach. Skatelios's men were slower and the gap began to widen.

Two more shots sounded and a sudden scream of agony made Callie spin round.

Lion Tattoo had run straight into one of the lethal-looking holes. His leg may have been broken because he was at an unnatural angle and writhing in agony. He started swearing angrily at Glass Eye. Glass Eye hesitated and then abandoned the chase to go back and help him.

'Yes!' shouted Nick in triumph.

'We should get off the beach,' panted Callie, after they'd been running for another ten minutes. 'We can be seen from too far away.'

They ran up a sand dune and left the sea behind them. There was a track leading further away through almond trees and then a vineyard. Callie stopped where waist-high vines were hanging with unripened grapes, and climbed over the low wall to hide.

It was the first chance they'd had to talk about what had happened.

'Do you think Mum and Dad are—' Nick couldn't quite produce the next word.

'Mum and Dad are fine,' Callie said firmly. 'Skatelios needs them if he's going to get to the keys *without* these.' She held up the four clay tablets she was still gripping in her hand.

'But they need those as well. That's what Dad was on about last night.'

Callie nodded. 'Yeah, but they've had three pieces of it for ages *and* they had a whole day to look at the fourth piece. They must have some idea where the keys are hidden.'

Nick popped a couple of the grapes into his mouth and then spat them out after one bite. 'Yuk!'

Callie rolled her eyes. 'How many times have I told you – they're not ripe yet.'

Nick ignored her question and asked his own, 'What do you think we should do?'

'Go to the police, obviously,' replied Callie.

'We can't do that! They'll arrest Dad.'

'I bet Dad'd rather be arrested than take his chances with Skatelios,' said Callie reasonably. 'The police don't break into your house by driving a car straight through the doors.'

Nick nodded. 'Okay. Obviously we should go to the police.'

'First though, we're going to bury the clay tablets.'

Nick looked bewildered. 'Why?'

'Because if we *are* caught by Skatelios, he can't do anything to us until we show him where they are.'

'Cool.'

'Look, get that stick.' Callie pointed at a curved tree branch on the ground that they could use as a spade. She checked the track beside the vineyard to see that no one was around, and then stood up.

The vines were planted in long equal rows. She started in the nearest corner and began to count along the first row. 'One... two... three... four... five... six...

seven... eight... nine...ten...' She stopped and turned at right angles to work her way through the rows. 'One... two... three... four... five... six... seven... eight... This one,' she selected the tenth vine in the eighth row. 'Go on. Get digging.'

It was hard going, as the ground was almost solid. Callie found another stick and began to dig as well.

'So our villa was right on top of King Akanon's Treasury?' Nick commented, as he excavated.

'Apparently,' said Callie. She wished she knew how her mum and dad had been getting under the villa.

'What's in the Treasury anyway?'

Callie raised an eyebrow. 'Treasure?'

Nick made a face. 'That could mean anything. Gold, jewels – even King Akanon's CD collection.'

'The legend says it was all the wealth of Thelta, collected over hundreds of years – so probably jewels and gold and other precious objects. There was even said to be a golden chariot and a golden ship.'

Nick glanced at his backpack. 'We're gonna need a bigger bag then.'

Between them they broke up the soil and made enough of a hole to bury the clay tablets in. Then they covered them over again and replaced the loose soil. The vine soon looked exactly as it had before – indistinguishable from any of the others.

'We need a way to remember the tenth vine in the eighth row...Or ten-eight,' said Nick, scratching his head.

'How about that it's the same date as my birthday?' suggested Callie.

'What is?'

'The tenth day of the eighth month.'

'Is it?'

Callie shook her head in disbelief. Brothers!

They arrived on the outskirts of Thelta Town, barely two hours after dawn, and found it was already busy. Cars and people were hurrying past them as Callie led the way through the suburbs, by hotels, and finally out onto the waterfront with its bars, cafés and colourful markets.

She had noticed the police station yesterday. It was on the harbour front right opposite the island's main ferry terminal.

'That way.' She pointed across a wide road busy with traffic. They were almost safe. As she started to cross, a strong hand wrenched her back painfully. Callie spun around in confusion and stared up into a face she knew only too well.

'Yiannis!' It was their gardener.

'Careful! Traffic drive on right in Thelta. You nearly walk in front of car.'

'Thank you,' said Callie, though she could have sworn there had been no car.

'What are you do here?' Yiannis wanted to know.

Before Callie could stop him, Nick blurted out they were escaping from someone called Skatelios who'd kidnapped their parents. 'He's after us because we've got—'

70

Callie almost lifted Nick off his feet. 'Come on, Nick. We need to get to the police station and tell *them* what's happened. I'm sure Yiannis understands.'

Yiannis nodded immediately. 'Police? Yes, yes, I take you to.'

Before Callie could argue, he was leading them across the road. She managed to shoot Nick an angry look, and place her finger over her mouth while Yiannis's back was turned.

The police station was barely another three-hundred metres on, housed in a modern building three storeys high.

Callie decided to try something. 'Yiannis, will you come inside with us in case we need an interpreter?'

Yiannis stopped as if he'd run into an invisible wall. 'No. They have peoples who talk English good. I get to work, yes?'

'Okay,' said Callie, and watched Yiannis practically run off, in the opposite direction to the police station. It was the first time she'd ever seen him in a hurry to work. That settled it. Yiannis was definitely not to be trusted, and Nick had just told him everything short of where they'd buried the clay tablets.

'Maybe he's wanted by the police for illegal lawn mowing,' suggested Nick.

'Let's hope that's all he's wanted for,' prayed Callie.

7
THE POLICE CHOOSE SIDES

They went into the police station, and explained their story to an English-speaking desk sergeant. When he'd written everything down, he ushered them into a small office.

It was almost as untidy as Nick's bedroom, only there were files and coffee cups scattered everywhere instead of clothes and computer games. There were also photographs of children, all of them younger than Callie and Nick, on the desk and on the walls. Whoever worked in this office had a large family.

After a moment, the door opened and a hawkish-looking man in his late forties ambled in. He propped the door open so he could see across the corridor to a much larger working area, where several officers were busy at their desks. 'I am Alekos Khrisous, of the Tourism Department of Thelta Police. I am here to help you,' he informed them.

He seemed unusually scruffy for someone with an important job. Even his hair was untidy, balding on top with the rest of it lank and overlong. It wasn't a look that was particularly flattering. He settled his overweight frame behind his desk.

'Please do not worry. I have sent officers to your home already – the Villa Limani, yes?'

Callie nodded, '*Efharisto* – thank you.'

'Now, tell me everything.'

This time Callie told the story – even about how her dad had come by King Akanon's map. When she got to the part about Skatelios threatening her parents at the taverna, Khrisous remained silent. He continued staring levelly at her. Callie didn't know why, but she left out the part about taking the clay tablets and burying them in the vineyard.

'You have been through a great ordeal,' concluded Khrisous, 'but now everything will be all right again.'

He gave them an encouraging smile and completely changed the subject.

'I have three daughters, aged two, nine and ten, and one son who is eight. I take them all swimming and sailing, and the two older girls have music and dancing lessons. I think my son will be football player. Do you like football?' He gazed expectantly at Nick.

Nick nodded and said his favourite team.

'Ah yes,' replied Khrisous, and named the team's most famous player.

'And what do you like doing?' he asked Callie.

Callie shrugged. Maybe he was trying to take her mind off what was happening to her parents, but it wasn't going to work. Before she could answer, the telephone rang, making her jump.

Khrisous lifted the receiver '*Yassu.*' It was the Greek term for hello, but then Callie didn't understand another word until Khrisous said, '*Efharisto*, thank you,' and rang off.

'As you reported – a car had been driven through the villa doors to gain entry. My officers also found the collapsed cellar wall which enabled you to escape. But I am afraid they did not find your parents.'

'Then he's taken them to his island!' Nick asserted.

'*He* being Mr Skatelios,' said Khrisous gravely. He sighed and tapped his fingertips together. 'Yet you did not see him at your villa.'

'But I had to fight off one of his gorillas last night,' exaggerated Nick.

'And another one of them tried to show us the short way down the mountain!' Callie said angrily. 'Don't you believe us?'

'*Again*,' said Khrisous slowly, 'you say you saw Mr Skatelios neither in the boat nor in the truck. You have no evidence...'

Callie almost shouted, '*But he threatened us all last night!*'

Khrisous took a long, deep breath. 'I will have one of our boats sent over to Skatelios Island, but I must state, this is against my better judgement.' He twisted in his seat and roared through the open door. 'MYKOS!' It sounded like a name.

A second later 'Mykos' came skidding into Khrisous's office. He was tall and thin and carrying a bulging black plastic bin liner. A two-way conversation in Greek, and seemingly about the bin liner, followed. Then Khrisous rattled out some orders and Mykos raced away.

'My officers collected some of your possessions. They

may be of use to you,' explained Khrisous, placing the black plastic bag on his desk.

'How did they know which was *our* stuff?' asked Nick suspiciously.

'They're detectives,' Khrisous replied simply.

He emptied the plastic bag. There were two backpacks (Callie's pink one and Nick's massive one), several items of clothing for both of them and their mobile phones.

'Thank you,' she said gratefully.

'The rest of your possessions will be returned to you when my men have finished searching your villa.'

'What are they searching it for?' demanded Nick.

'Evidence...clues...'

Callie half wondered if Khrisous had ordered his men to find the clay tablets. Well, they wouldn't find them in a hurry.

Khrisous clapped his hands.

'Now, how about breakfast?'

Callie had eaten only one slice of toast. Nick, on the other hand, had eaten almost everything on the police station canteen menu, including: *giaourtopita ke meli,* sheep's milk yoghurt with thyme-flavoured honey, and *tiropitta,* warm pastries filled with feta cheese.

They had learned almost everything there was to learn about Alekos Khrisous, whose four children were called Maria, Anna, Elena, and Stevi. He had once been based in Athens, but now preferred the slower pace of Thelta. His dog was called Demis, (Nick thought he'd said Dennis), and it followed him to work every day and slept outside in the yard! And his name, Khrisous, meant gold in English. Eventually he ran out of things to tell them about himself, and took them back to his office. He left them there waiting for news from Skatelios Island.

They didn't have to wait long.

'It's Skatelios!' gasped Callie, putting her hand to her mouth.

She was looking right through Khrisous's open office door into the larger working space beyond. Standing talking to Khrisous, as if he was his favourite son, was the self-appointed king of Thelta, Georgíou Skatelios.

'I think I'm going to be sick,' said Nick.

'Do you think they've arrested him?' Skatelios couldn't possibly have heard Callie, yet he took that moment to stare into the office, directly at her.

She shivered as if a large spider had crawled over her skin.

Skatelios turned back to Khrisous and gave him a wide smile.

'What's going off?' Callie said angrily. 'They look like best friends, not like policeman and arrested criminal.' The two men were shaking hands; not an ordinary handshake – Skatelios was holding Khrisous's hand warmly in his hands and then embracing him.

After more smiles all round, Khrisous returned to his office. This time he slammed the door loudly behind him. Callie felt as if she and Nick had been summoned to the headmaster's office – and the headmaster was about to go ballistic.

'Mr Skatelios has cooperated with us fully. He has permitted us to search both his home *and* his island, and, I can categorically assure you that your parents are *not* there.'

Callie said nothing. Given what she'd just seen between Khrisous and Skatelios she would have been surprised to hear anything else.

Khrisous opened his window and seemed to calm down. 'We still have two lines of investigation of course. The man sailing the boat and the man driving the truck, both of whom reappeared at your villa this morning. I will ask a colleague to go through anything you remember about the boat, the truck and the cars they were driving this morning.' His voice softened significantly. 'I'm sure this line of enquiry will lead us to your parents.'

Or not, thought Callie. You're obviously working for Skatelios.

Khrisous started playing with his car keys. 'You said that your parents miraculously had the entire King Akanon map. What happened to it?'

'I don't know,' lied Callie. Skatelios had obviously told him *they* had it.

'What do you want to know about that for?' asked Nick bluntly.

'Because all four pieces belong to the Theltan government,' Khrisous reminded him.

Nick looked down at his feet to avoid Khrisous's hawk-like stare, but Khrisous changed the subject. 'I'm going to make arrangements for you to be placed with one of my officers until your parents are found.'

Nick leapt up. 'What? What for?'

Callie shook her head at him. 'Because we can't stay at the villa on our own, Nick.'

'WHY NOT!'

'Because those men, who are obviously nothing to do with Skatelios, might come back.' Callie tried to make Nick shut up by the expression on her face.

After a pause, Khrisous stood up. 'I will speak to Officer Papadopoulos about settling you with him.'

'What are you playing at?' Nick shouted at Callie, as soon as Khrisous had gone. 'We can't help Mum and Dad if we're stuck with Officer Propercrapolis.'

'That's why we're getting out of here,' said Callie. 'If the police aren't going to help Mum and Dad, we are.'

She was already jamming the back of her chair under the door handle to stop it being opened. She ran to the window, pushed it wide open and leaned out. They were at least one floor up, though right below Khrisous's office was a long, flat roof belonging to a Portakabin.

Callie pulled a second chair under the windowsill and turned to Nick. 'You go first.'

'What?'

'We've got to do this quickly, Nick!'

'All right!' He climbed onto the chair and then up onto the windowsill. 'We're really high!'

'Hurry up!'

Gingerly, Nick put one foot outside and began to climb out backwards, gripping the frame tightly.

Callie climbed onto the windowsill behind him. 'Now climb down,' she ordered.

Nick looked down. 'It's too far.'

'Then you'll have to hang and drop.'

'I'm not Spiderman, you know!'

Callie gripped Nick's wrists. 'Look, I've got you and I won't let go until you're ready.'

Nick weighed it up for a minute and then nodded. 'You'd better not drop me.'

Still facing into the office and grasping the windowsill, Nick let his feet slide down the outside wall until the toes of his trainers slotted into a groove between bricks. Callie was still hanging onto him as his face became level with the bottom of the window.

'How much further is it?' Nick wanted to know, unable to see the Portakabin roof from the angle he was at.

'Not nearly as far as you jumped from the boat last night,' Callie encouraged.

'That's easy,' said Nick confidently. 'Let me go then.'

'All right. On the count of three...One...Two—'

Nick slipped out of her fingers.

'OWWW! What happened to *three*?' Nick shouted up from the Portakabin roof.

Callie was staring at the office door. Someone had tried to open it and now they were banging on it.

'What's going on in there?' It was Khrisous's voice.

Then a moment later Callie heard him shout: 'MYKOS!' and something in Greek. He must be ordering Mykos to cut them off outside. Then he was banging on the office door again. It sounded as if he was putting his shoulder to it.

Callie snatched up the black bin liner and climbed through the window. She paused on the ledge to get her balance – she could easily sprain an ankle if she hit the roof beneath her badly. She leapt. As she landed she allowed her legs to buckle and cushion the impact, and ended up in a squatting position.

'That was amazing,' enthused Nick, looking really impressed. 'But you still dropped me.'

'Khrisous was trying to get in!'

Callie scrambled up and started looking for a way to get to the ground. She spotted it in the shape of a green rubbish skip full of bulging plastic bags. It was right beside the Portakabin.

'We need to jump into that!' She pointed. 'Those bags'll break our fall.'

'How do you know that?' shrieked Nick. 'They could have broken bottles in them or... bricks.'

'Yes! Because everyone throws broken bottles and bricks away in plastic bags, don't they?' said Callie sarcastically. 'Look!' She pointed at one of the plastic bags which had burst open. Shreds of paper were spilling out. 'It's shredded paper.'

'WAIT!' It was from above them. Khrisous had forced his office door open and was hanging out of the window.

'Just do what I do,' yelled Callie, and leapt into the green skip. It was like jumping straight onto a bed, yielding and soft. Nick jumped after her and then they were climbing out of the skip and breaking into a run. Mykos came pelting out of the police station after them.

8
THE FORTRESS OF ATHETOS

They lost Mykos in a crowd of English tourists streaming off the mid-morning passenger ferry. They attached themselves to a bunch of kids their own age and walked straight past him, hiding the black plastic bag between them. In Khrisous's office, Mykos had barely glanced at their faces.

Callie tried to think as they hurried through the maze of streets taking them further and further away from the police station. Now they weren't just on the run from Skatelios and his tattooed psychos, they were also escaping from the police. How could they possibly rescue their parents? They were two kids in a foreign country with no money and no one to help them. Everything they had was contained in a Greek bin liner!

'I'm not going any further.' Nick had stopped right in the middle of the street. People were having to walk round him.

'What?'

'I'm not going any further until you tell me *where* we're going.'

Callie gaped at her brother in exasperation. 'I don't know, Nick, where do you suggest we go?'

'Why don't we go back to the villa?'

'Because it's the first place everybody will look for us,' said Callie, shaking her head.

'Well, what *are* we going to do then?'

'I don't *know!*' admitted Callie. 'I'm not Mum and Dad.'

She looked round. They couldn't have chosen a worse place for an argument. It was a very un-touristy part of town. The shops here were normal, everyday shops like grocers and hardware stores, none of them selling souvenirs or postcards. Not one of the signs had an English translation underneath, as they did in the areas popular with visitors.

A Greek lady, dressed all in black and older even than Callie's grandmother, was sitting outside a café watching them. She smiled and started speaking in Greek. For all Callie knew, she was giving them fashion tips or the latest gossip from the Greek version of *EastEnders,* neither of which seemed likely.

'What's *her* problem?' asked Nick.

The Greek lady had started saying the same word over and over. '*Xenothohio*...? *Xenothohio*...? *Xenothohio*...?' Then she pointed down the street to where they could see another road and added, '*Xenothohio.*'

'Xenothohio. Xenothohio,' repeated Callie.

'Don't you start!' said Nick.

'I'm sure I know that word... "Hotel"!' Callie said in a sudden brainwave. 'There must be a hotel up there and she thinks we're lost.'

'It's obviously the suitcase,' said Nick.

Callie looked confused. 'What suitcase?'

Nick pointed at the black plastic bag she was carrying.

He nodded pleasantly to the Greek lady. 'Hotel-zenothingy.'

Callie thought about it. The Greek lady was right. They were lost, completely lost, and a hotel was the perfect place to go. It would be full of tourists, and two English kids wouldn't stand out at all. They could hang around there until they worked out what to do.

She smiled at the Greek lady and said, '*Efharisto. Efharisto.* Thank you.'

The Greek lady pointed at her own silver hair and then at Nick's blond hair, and started speaking again.

'She's having a go at my hair now!'

'It's because you're blond. You know the Greeks think it means you're blessed by the gods.'

'If this is her idea of being blessed by the gods, she's bonkers,' said Nick.

'Just smile and let's go.'

They both smiled and headed down the alley to the Xenothohio.

Hotel Thelta looked brand new and stood just on the edge of town, close to a beach with pink-tinged sand. It was big, easily the biggest building they'd seen in Thelta Town, and like most of the buildings on the island, was painted white. Right across the front there was a semi-circle of lush, green grass dotted with apricot and pear trees.

A hotel *was* the perfect place to hide. There was so much coming and going of holiday-makers all the time, the Greek staff could hardly be expected to remember each face. Adults never remembered kids anyway unless they were kicking off; if you were quiet and well-behaved, grown-ups just ignored you.

'Act as if you live here,' Callie advised, as they went through the revolving doors. 'Oh, I forgot, you always do that wherever you are.'

Nick grinned at her. It was the first time he'd looked happy all morning.

Inside the spacious lobby there were mostly English tourists, chatting or heading out to the beach.

'We ought to change,' said Callie. 'The police *and* Skatelios's men will be looking for us dressed like this.'

'Good of Khrisous to give us our clothes, so we could throw him off our trail then,' said Nick.

Callie pointed at a sign which read: SWIMMING POOL. 'There's bound to be changing rooms.' She was right. There were separate areas for men and women. Callie split the contents of the black plastic bag and went into the women's area. She stepped into the first cubicle she came to and locked the door.

After changing into a different top and shorts, she looked to see what else she'd got in her backpack. There was her mobile phone, the postcards she'd bought yesterday, sun cream, half a bottle of water (warm), *The History of Thelta*, and three euros and twenty cents. Two pounds wouldn't get them very far, and it was really unlikely Nick had any money. He always relied on the Bank of Mum and Dad.

Callie sat down on the cubicle's wooden seat, applying sun cream and savouring being alone for a few minutes. It was unexpectedly comforting to have Nick on her side, but also worrying. Now she had to take responsibility for both of them, and this was hardly 'Keep an eye on your brother while you're at McDonalds.' This could easily end up 'Try not to get your brother killed.' Callie wasn't sure she could guarantee that.

She realised that silent tears were running down her cheeks. She dashed them away angrily and vowed, I'm not going to let *anyone* harm Nick; not anyone.

She was folding everything away, including the plastic bag when her backpack started to ring. Or at least the mobile phone inside it did. Panicking, Callie rummaged around till she found it and then stared at the screen. It read: MUM CALLING.

Callie jabbed at the 'talk' key. 'Mum!'

'No...a friend.' It was a man's voice speaking in an American accent – Skatelios!

Callie felt sick. Her thumb hovered over the 'disconnect' key.

'Don't hang up,' came the hated voice again, as if Skatelios was actually watching her. 'Just listen.'

With a shaking hand, Callie put the mobile phone to her ear.

After a pause, Skatelios continued, 'Good girl...your parents are safe and unharmed.'

Callie wanted to sob with relief. She swallowed the lump in her throat and carried on listening.

'All I want is the clay tablets. Bring them to me and your parents will go free. Do you understand?'

'Yes.' Callie was shocked at how tiny her voice sounded. She swallowed again and said in a stronger voice, 'I want to talk to them.'

There was a long silence on the other end of the line and then, miraculously: 'Callie, darling, Dad and I are all right, just tell Mr Skatelios where the clay tablets are and then stay out of the way. We'll find you when he lets us—'

Her mum was cut off abruptly.

'No. That is not the way it will happen. You and your brother will bring the clay tablets in person. Do you understand?'

'Yes,' confirmed Callie. 'Where?'

'On the coastal road, three kilometres from Thelta Town, is the village of Athetos. There on a small island connected to the headland lie the ruins of a fortress.'

'Yes, I've heard of it,' said Callie. It was on one of the postcards in her backpack.

'You will be there at seven this evening with the clay tablets, and then you will be reunited with your mother and your father. Do you under—'

Callie cut him off. 'Yes, I understand.'

'You took your time,' Nick greeted her as she came out of the changing rooms. 'Why do girls always take so long?'

'I've been speaking to Mum...'

Nick stared at her open-mouthed. 'You're kidding!'

'She's all right, Nick, and so's Dad...I spoke to Skatelios as well.'

'How?'

'On my mobile. They phoned me.'

'How did they know you'd got your mobile?'

Callie raised an eyebrow. 'Can't you guess?'

'Khrisous! I bet he told his mate Skatelios,' sneered Nick in disgust.

Callie nodded. 'Skatelios wants to trade Mum and Dad for the clay tablets. We've got to meet him here.' She showed him the postcard of the ruined fortress.

'We can't trust him, Callie,' said Nick immediately.

'That's why we need to find a souvenir shop.'

Nick frowned. 'A souvenir shop? What are you going to do – buy him a present?'

'That's exactly what I'm going to do...And by the way, you've got your T-shirt on inside out.'

They didn't have to go far to find a souvenir shop. There was one right on the beach in front of the hotel. Callie had guessed right: they sold nearly all the same things at these shops: inflatable turtles, beach towels with Thelta written on them, and just what she was looking for—

'A souvenir King Akanon's treasure map!' Nick's mouth fell open. 'NO! You can't be serious!'

'If Skatelios tries to cheat us we'll still have the *real* map to bargain with. And if everything goes okay, we can ring him when we're safe and tell him where the real map is.'

Nick raised his hand, palm upwards for a high five.

Callie slapped it. 'The only problem is that the souvenir map costs ten euros, and I've only got three,' she said, looking at the souvenir.

'I'll get it,' said Nick, delving into the pocket of his fresh shorts.

He drew out a large, screwed-up bundle of euros in notes of every denomination: tens, twenties, fifties and even some hundreds.

Callie dragged him and the money to the corner of the shop where they couldn't be overlooked. 'Where did you get all that?' It seemed Nick had his own secret treasury.

'You remember that vase thing the clay tablets were hidden in?'

'Yes?' frowned Callie.

'Well, there was another one, and I wondered: if one of them opened, maybe the other one did as well. And while you were watching Skatelios's men, I found all this money.'

Callie stared at her brother in astonishment. 'Mum and Dad's piggy bank. I overheard them talking about it but didn't know where it was.'

'I didn't think Dad'd want Skatelios to have it,' Nick said reasonably.

Callie giggled and threw her arms around him.

'Get off!'

'Blessed by the gods!'

The fortress of Athetos was built on an island connected to the rest of Thelta by a strip of rock, making it look like the head of a gigantic spoon. Nine wide round towers with a pattern of outward jutting battlements were linked together by solid-looking stone walls. The distance right around the fortress must have been more than a kilometre. They had used some of Nick's stash of euros to hire a taxi to get there.

'Athetos Fortress was built in 1492 AD, when the Venetians ruled Thelta, to guard the seaways against Ottoman invaders and pirate ships,' Callie read from *The History of Thelta,* as the taxi rumbled along.

'A bit after King Akanon then,' observed Nick.

'Mmm...You'll like this bit – it's been closed to the public since 1983, because an earthquake made the walls start to collapse.'

'Brilliant!'

The taxi stopped beside the rock causeway leading to the fortress. Callie started to climb out.

'Is dangerous!' The taxi driver pointed at the fortress, looking worried.

You don't know the half of it, thought Callie, but said, 'It's okay, we're meeting someone. *Near* it, not *on* it.'

'Is closed,' the taxi driver reiterated.

When Callie just nodded and smiled pleasantly, he shrugged and started turning his taxi round to head back to Thelta Town. They watched him drive away into the pine-clad hills, the afternoon heat creating a quivering haze on the horizon.

'He's got a point,' said Nick. 'Skatelios is probably planning to drop one of those dodgy walls right on top of us.'

Callie chewed her lip. 'No wonder he wants to meet us here. It's dangerous, closed to the public, and there's no way we can get over there without him seeing us.'

The causeway to the island was blocked by two serious-looking aluminium gates stitched together with razor wire.

'Got the key?' asked Nick.

'We don't need it,' replied Callie, looking at the thick chain which had been holding the gates together – it was sliced right through.

'Well, at least we know they're here.'

'And I bet they know we're here.' Callie opened the gates and slipped through. Her heart rate quickened significantly. 'Come on, let's get on with it.'

They began to cross the causeway with heavy feet. It couldn't possibly have felt more like a trap. At the other end, the island climbed steeply and the remains of a footpath angled off across loose, stony ground.

Nick looked up at the fortress walls. 'Do you think Lion Tattoo and Glass Eye are in there?'

'I don't know. Lion Tattoo hurt himself on the beach, didn't he?' said Callie.

'Good! I hope he broke his leg.'

'But Glass Eye wouldn't stay away if Skatelios paid him. He loves his work too much. There were two other men at the villa as well – the smartly dressed one, and I heard someone else upstairs as well!'

'So we're probably outnumbered,' Nick grinned weakly.

'Probably.'

They set off on the narrow path that angled away from the causeway. It was barely wider than Callie's foot, yet was etched deeply into the rock and vegetation. The hills all over Thelta were carved with similar tracks, made by the domesticated goats that roamed the island. Sometimes you'd never even see the goats, just hear a tinkling sound from their bells. Somebody must keep their goats at the fortress.

'This way,' said Callie, taking a detour from the path. They were short of the fortress gate, a giant archway set between two square towers with a courtyard visible beyond. 'Maybe we'll find a way in they're not expecting,' she added.

They followed a second goat track which curved upwards around the hill and started running right along the bottom of the fortress wall. Halfway around they found a damaged section of wall. A finger-width crack, starting at ground level, was a hand-width gap halfway up the wall and wide enough to climb through at the top. Whoever looked after the fortress had tried to prevent any further collapse by building steel scaffolding around the damage.

'It's like a climbing frame!' said Callie excitedly. 'But we have to be quick. When we don't come in through the main gate they're bound to start looking for us out here.'

They clambered onto the first 'rung' of the scaffolding. Callie stretched for the horizontal pole above her and pulled herself up. Nick followed. They continued climbing until they reached a small wooden platform where somebody had been working to repair the wall; there were some stonemason's tools about, a mallet and a chisel.

Callie could see right through the crack in the wall. There must once have been buildings inside the fortress – but all that remained were ruins overgrown with long, straw-like grass and the occasional blade-shaped cypress tree.

Incongruously, on a stone platform at the top of some wide steps was a large yellow and blue sun umbrella, with a table and canvas chairs arranged beneath it. Three people were sitting at the table as if they were out for an afternoon's picnic. It was her mum, her dad, and the man who had kidnapped them: Georgiou Skatelios.

Callie was on the verge of tears. This morning she had wondered if she would ever see her parents again. Now here they were. They were all right and she could rescue them.

'It's Mum and Dad,' blurted Nick. 'And Skatelios!'

Callie shushed him hurriedly. She had heard footsteps crunching up the same goat path they'd used. She put a finger to her mouth and pointed. The smartly dressed man was walking towards the scaffolding.

Callie and Nick flattened themselves face down against the wooden platform, and Callie put her eye to a gap between the planking. Smartly Dressed Man marched right underneath without glancing up. He carried on walking until he was out of sight. Callie blew out her cheeks in relief. That had been close. She peered through the split in the wall again, not sure what she should do next. Mum and Dad looked anxious, but otherwise okay.

After a few minutes, Smartly Dressed Man returned from his sweep of the fortress's outer walls, and Callie saw him go straight to Skatelios. He shrugged and turned his hands palms upwards.

'He's saying he couldn't find us,' interpreted Nick.

Skatelios erupted from his seat and struck Smartly Dressed Man hard across the face. Smartly Dressed Man was sent spinning backwards and sprawling onto the steps.

Callie gasped. Before now she'd imagined that Skatelios left all the violence to Glass Eye and Lion Tattoo. As she continued to watch, Skatelios produced a mobile phone from his suit pocket and flipped it open. Even before he pressed the key, Callie knew who he was calling. She desperately tried to snatch her own mobile from her backpack.

'What's up?' Nick looked startled. *'What's up?'*

It was too late. Callie's distinctive ringtone was already playing – pinpointing exactly where they were like a fanfare.

9
LION TATTOO

There was no going back now. Callie stood up on the platform and squeezed through the crack in the ramparts. She came out onto a narrow stone walkway inside the fortress.

Skatelios was a little way in front of her and a long way down. She spotted Lion Tattoo, loitering under an archway she hadn't been able to see before. He hadn't broken his leg after all. More alarmingly, Glass Eye was standing on the same walkway as her, and he was only a short sprint away.

'You have found the back door once again,' Skatelios complimented her, his voice echoing off the fortress walls.

'Do whatever he says, Callie,' shouted her dad. 'It'll soon be over.'

The emotions were building inside Callie more than ever. She wanted to run to her parents and let them take control, let them make everything be all right again but she couldn't allow herself to be weak. She couldn't trust this evil man.

'STOP!' Callie was surprised at how strong her voice sounded when her stomach was in her mouth. Glass Eye had taken a stride towards her, but now he hesitated.

Callie snatched the souvenir clay tablets from her backpack and threatened to hurl them at the stone floor below, where they would smash into unreadable crumbs.

'STOP!' Skatelios repeated the word. Glass Eye froze.

'Let my mum and dad go,' Callie shouted at Skatelios. 'Let them go through the gate and then I'll give him the map.' She indicated Glass Eye.

Skatelios thought fast and then nodded to Callie's parents. Without further prompting they started moving quickly toward the gateway. When they had passed under the archway, Callie returned the clay tablets to her backpack and fastened it. She threw the backpack to Glass Eye, who caught it clumsily in his scrawny arms and continued towards her.

'BRING IT TO ME!' Skatelios flung up at him angrily. '*Then* kill them.'

Callie stared down into the courtyard. Grinning unpleasantly, Lion Tattoo pushed her parents back through the arch with the barrel of a shotgun. She had been right not to trust Skatelios with the real map, but she had still walked straight into his trap.

Skatelios aimed a kick at Smartly Dressed Man. 'You! Go after the girl! Find the boy.'

Callie already had one foot back through the crack in the wall and was squeezing through as Glass Eye reached Skatelios. As she stumbled out onto the scaffolding, she heard Skatelios's cry of rage:

'THIS ISN'T THE MAP!'

She could imagine the frenzy going off inside the fortress. Any minute now Skatelios's men would fall upon her from above, and from the gateway!

And Nick was gone!

'Nick!'

'I'm down here.'

He'd been busy while she'd been inside the fortress. He'd climbed down and found a loose steel pole from the scaffolding. Then he'd jammed it into the crack at the base of the damaged wall and was levering it backwards and forwards. Callie realised immediately what he was doing. They could stop at least one of Skatelios's men pursuing them.

She scrambled down the scaffolding like a monkey, and added her weight to the pole. Smartly Dressed Man had pushed his thick frame into the break in the wall. It was a much tighter fit than it had been for Callie, and he was already struggling.

Then there was a cracking sound and the wall started to give. Seconds later and it was collapsing into the fortress, taking Smartly Dressed Man with it. An immense crash shook the ground and raised a cloud of dust.

It was a small victory but Callie and Nick still had Skatelios and the rest of his men to contend with. Callie led the charge down the goat track, causing a mini-landslide. If they could get to the strip of land which connected the island to the rest of Thelta first... Before they made even a quarter of the way, they saw Skatelios, hurrying ahead to cut them off.

Callie managed to stop her headlong rush. 'We have to try another way.'

'There aren't any!' Nick shouted back, almost falling over her.

'Just come on!'

Callie headed off again, back in the direction they'd come from, though at a lower angle, away from the fortress. Her only thought was to put some distance between them and Skatelios's men.

Nick was right – there weren't any other ways off the island. All around her Callie could see only bare rocks and scrub, leading down to the sea. Water on three sides of the fortress was better than a ten-foot high wall!

Then, halfway around, they came to a wide area of bushes spreading across the hillside. Scant as the bushes were, they were the only hiding place they'd seen so far. Callie dived straight into them and dropped to her hands and knees.

An explosion of hair, horns and bells came flying at her. Callie bit down a scream, then realised it was a goat panicking as its own hiding place was invaded. It hurtled past and kept on running until it was out of sight, and all that remained was the sound of its tinkling bell.

Tinkling bell...Callie's eyes widened in horror. Her mobile phone! She snatched it out of her pocket in terror and stabbed at the key to mute it. A second after the icon of a crossed-out speaker appeared on the screen, a message flashed up: MUM CALLING.

Callie and Nick looked at each other in relief. They had almost been caught again.

'Where's *your* phone?' Callie demanded.

Nick showed her his lifeless Nokia. 'Have you got a charger?'

Callie sighed. 'We can't stay here. Sooner or later they'll search the bushes.'

'We could swim for it,' tried Nick hesitantly.

Callie stomach turned over. 'I'd rather take my chances with Lion Tattoo.'

'Well, I wouldn't . . .' said Nick.

Callie peeped out from the bushes. They weren't far from the edge of the island. She could hear the sea lapping softly against the rocks below. If they were lucky, they could make it all the way to the edge without leaving cover.

'There has to be another way!' Callie was desperate. 'Maybe there's a way to walk around the side of the island without going into the water.' But she'd seen from the fortress ramparts the way the natural rock fell into deep water right around the island – apart from along the causeway. Deep water. The very words terrified her.

'I can help you, Callie. It'll be all right.' Nick was still trying to convince her.

CRACK! It was single loud sound, and Callie registered immediately that it was a gunshot. She raised her head slightly and looked back at the fortress. There was no sign of Skatelios *or* his men.

'They've shot Mum and Dad!' Nick shouted.

Callie grabbed him before he could burst out of the bushes.

'No! Look!' She pointed. Glass Eye had come round the hill, and was prodding a dead goat with his foot. 'He must have heard it and thought it was us.' Or just killed it for fun, she added to herself. She looked at her brother's worried face and made up her mind. He was a strong swimmer: maybe he could help her, maybe he couldn't – but at least he'd have a chance of saving himself.

'Okay, we'll swim for it,' said Callie. Her lip was trembling.

They worked their way through the bushes on hands and knees to where the rocks slid alarmingly away to an almost vertical plunge into black water.

'How deep do you think it is?'

'I don't think it's the shallow end,' replied Nick quietly.

Callie nodded. She didn't think so either.

'Have you still got that plastic bag the police gave us our stuff in?' asked Nick.

Callie stared at him in confusion. 'Why? What do you want that for?'

'If we fill it with air you could use it as a float.'

Callie smiled briefly and produced the neatly folded black plastic bag from one of her pockets.

'You *folded* it!'

'Just get on with it!' Callie ordered, a hint of embarrassment in her voice.

Nick opened the bag, dragged it through the air to inflate it and then started to twist the opening to trap the air inside.

'Wait. Where's the money and your mobile phone?'

Nick gave her a quizzical look.

'We can put them inside the bag to keep them dry.'

Nick untwisted the bag and started dumping screwed-up bundles of euros into it. Then his phone. Callie dropped hers in too.

'Okay,' she said.

Nick filled the bag with air again and twisted the top tightly. 'We need to tie it with something.' He searched his pockets and found a piece of string. A distant shout made him hurry: Skatelios's men had discovered the bushes and started to search.

Callie crawled to the sloping rock and walked herself forward to the very edge on her bottom – using the palms of her hands and her feet. She dangled her feet over the water, almost her own height below her.

'Here.' Nick reached forward and handed her the makeshift buoyancy aid. 'Let me go first though. Then I can help you.'

Before Callie could argue Nick was sliding confidently down the rock and dropping straight into the water. There was a splash, and his head surfaced almost immediately. He was grinning.

'Is it cold?' Callie asked.

'Freezing.'

Callie wanted another moment to compose herself but she could hear Lion Tattoo and Glass Eye shouting to one other and beating the bushes behind her. She took a deep breath, pushed off with her hands, and plunged.

She went under, immediately losing her grip on the plastic bag. She snatched at handfuls of water and kicked for the surface. Although there was no sound, she was screaming in terror inside her head. She was going to be sucked further and further under the water like before. Then barely a second later her face was above the rippling surface and she was drawing in air gratefully, and feeling the shock of the cold sea.

She began to tread water, working her legs up and down and circling her arms. Nick was beside her and forcing the inflated bag back into her hand. Her panic subsided. She was swimming.

'Follow me,' Nick said, splashing away with a confident crawl stroke, rocking his body so that he could lift first one arm and then the other out of the water. He stopped every few strokes to look back and check she was okay.

Callie found she was able to keep up with him by holding the float out in front of her and kicking her legs. The effort even began to take away the sting of the cold water.

They had been swimming for several minutes before she heard more shouting. She didn't need to look back to realise that either Lion Tattoo or Glass Eye had spotted them in the water. She expected to hear another gunshot at any second and feel the...Callie didn't know what it felt like to be shot, and she didn't want to find out either. She kicked her legs even harder than before.

'Look!' Nick was floating on his back, waiting for her to catch up.

Callie turned her body slightly in the swelling water to see what Nick was staring at. She was far enough offshore to see the whole side of the island. Both Lion Tattoo and Glass Eye were running across the hill towards the causeway. Glass Eye had a mobile phone to his ear, probably informing Skatelios they'd gone into the water. Now they'd never be able to swim round to the mainland without being cut off. But they still had to try.

'Keep going, and don't wait for me,' Callie instructed Nick.

'No way!' replied Nick. 'You've got all the money in that bag.'

Even in her despair, Callie managed a smile.

They started swimming again, following the ragged outline of rocks. Maybe, just maybe they'd reach the headland before Skatelios did. Except... Callie's legs were beginning to tire. She was still kicking, but was moving more slowly.

It was barely another minute before she heard the engines. Motorboat engines! A sleek, white craft like the blade of a knife came slicing through the waves towards them. Any fleeting hope that it had no interest in them dissolved as the name along the gleaming side became visible: *Skatelios*, and in Roman numerals *III*.

It carved through the water so close to Callie that a wall of foam came rushing at her. She went under momentarily, to come up coughing and spluttering and being driven back towards the rocks around the island. She bobbed up and down in the churning water. *Skatelios III* was making a rapid circle in the sea. It faced her and Nick again and speared straight at them. Callie could make out a muscular figure at the wheel. Lion Tattoo!

Callie looked at the rocks again. There was a gap in them she hadn't noticed before – a cavernous, gaping hole. A cave extended right underneath the fortress island.

'Aim for that cave,' she gasped. There was nowhere else for them to go.

They began swimming for their lives, every second the scream of motorboat engines getting closer and closer. The onward rush of the motorboat created another wave. It funnelled between the rocks at the mouth of the cave, gathered momentum like a mini tidal wave, and thrust them forward on its crest like body surfers.

Five seconds and they were inside the cave and the motorboat was still outside. Lion Tattoo reversed the motorboat's engines and started testing the depth of the water with an oar.

Exhausted but still afloat, Callie rapidly scanned the cave for a way of escape. There wasn't one. No convenient tunnel or steps leading to the outside world. There wasn't even anywhere they could climb out of the water. The cave was a big dome with the sea lapping against its sides.

Then, unaccountably, Callie felt something solid beneath her feet. She stretched out a toe under the water: there it was again.

She looked above her. A huge section of rock was missing. It must have collapsed and fallen straight into the water where it was now lying completely submerged.

Callie swam a little further and let her feet touch bottom again. Yes, she was right. It made the water shallower at just that point. She worked her way right along the sunken rock until she found a large section that was completely flat, and only half a metre under the water. She was able to stand up. Then just as abruptly the rock fell away again and she plunged back into deep water.

Outside, Lion Tattoo was losing his patience. They could hear him gunning the motorboat's engines like he was revving up a car.

'Nick, swim over to me quickly. Don't climb out on the rock, swim round it.'

'I get it,' said Nick immediately, and struck out for her. He made it with only seconds to spare. *Skatelios III* came powering towards them, like a shimmering missile fired through the water.

A heartbeat and then a terrific, grating, tearing metal sound as the motorboat ploughed straight into the submerged rock. For a brief second a look of confusion clouded Lion Tattoo's expression – the water was deep, the kids were swimming!

Then the motorboat grounded itself completely and its forward momentum was arrested. Lion Tattoo was slung over the low Perspex cockpit. He landed in the water with a splash behind Callie and Nick, but they were already swimming for the mouth of the cave.

As they emerged it seemed slightly darker. The sky was infused with gold, the remains of the day's sunlight. In their effort to escape, they'd failed to realise dusk was coming on.

Callie's gaze was caught by a small red and yellow

fishing boat barely a kilometre offshore, and a fisherman lowering a weighted lobster pot into the water. Their friend Manolis, from The Grapes taverna! He worked his way down the coast every evening emptying lobster pots and turning in his catch at his dad's taverna.

'MANOLIS!' gurgled Nick. 'If we can get to his boat—'

'He's too far out to help us,' gasped Callie. Swimming to the cave had used up every last ounce of her strength.

'We have to try,' panted Nick.

Callie mustered a nod. 'Okay… You take the bag.'

'But—'

'I've still got some strength in my arms,' Callie explained.

Nick reached for the makeshift float, and they started to swim again. They began to make headway, very slowly at first and then as soon as they were clear of the cave opening, the current began to take them further out, miraculously towards Manolis's boat.

Manolis had finished re-setting the lobster pot. Now he was pulling the starter cord on his outboard engine, and Callie heard it cough back into life.

'Manolis! Manolis!' cried Nick, finding a shout left in him.

Callie groaned. Manolis was too far away to hear, and he probably couldn't see their heads in the water. He was turning his boat away to head further along the coast.

Then suddenly, something made him look directly at them: something shattering. An explosion had ripped apart the peace of the Theltan sunset. Callie twisted around. A ball of flame and thick black smoke burst from the cave mouth.

'Lion Tattoo's boat's blown up!' Nick said excitedly.

Callie tried to think. That was all it could be. Maybe the collision with the submerged rock had caused a petrol leak and Lion Tattoo used a lighter to see what damage there was . . . Or maybe he'd tried to restart the engine and a stray spark had set off the petrol. Whatever had happened, he wouldn't be aiming *Skatelios III* at kids swimming in the sea again!

Callie couldn't feel any sense of victory, only that it was one less enemy for them to deal with. And Manolis had changed direction and was closing in on them. Callie wished he would go faster. Skatelios, Glass Eye and Smartly Dressed Man were still out there, and they could hardly have failed to hear that explosion. They might be on their way in other boats – maybe *Skatelios I* and *Skatelios II*.

'Callie! Niko!' Manolis was dumbfounded. He cut the boat's engine and guided it carefully beside them. 'What happened? Has there been an accident? Such an explosion!'

Callie reached up for the side of Manolis's boat and clung on. 'Manolis, listen to me. We're being chased. It's the same people who tried to kidnap Nick. One of their boats hit a rock and blew up.' She paused for Manolis to take it all in. 'They may have other boats and if they have, that explosion is bound to bring them here.'

Manolis understood immediately. 'Then climb in as

107

quickly as you can. I will take you to safety.' Manolis wasn't giving a thought to his *own* safety.

'I don't think I can climb in,' gasped Callie. 'I feel like my arms are going to drop off.'

Manolis helped first Callie and then Nick over the side of his boat. He hid them quickly beneath some tarpaulin and old netting, and continued on his way as if nothing had happened. Barely moments later, Callie heard the sinister sound of motorboat engines. She peeped out from under the tarpaulin.

Apart from the slight difference in name, *Skatelios II* was identical to *Skatelios III* – stylish and lean and built for speed. It pulled up alongside Manolis's boat, thudding into it.

'Have you seen two children swimming?' the boat driver asked. There was a hint of a Greek accent, but he was speaking in English.

'I have seen nothing but empty lobster pots all evening,' Manolis replied.

'Lobster pots! Didn't you hear the explosion?' said the other, sounding astonished.

'An *explosion*?' exclaimed Manolis.

'Are you *deaf*? They must have heard it as far away as Athens.'

Under the edge of the tarpaulin, Callie saw Manolis remove an earpiece and then wave an iPod at the man questioning him. Good one, she thought. She carefully pulled the tarpaulin further over her until she could no longer see Manolis.

'Never mind.' The motorboat driver must have decided he was wasting his time, because Callie heard the revving of engines, and then Manolis's boat bobbed up and down on a violent wave. The sound of the motorboat receded.

Callie risked another peep. *Skatelios II* was speeding towards the cave, where smoke was still pouring out.

Manolis got his boat under way again. It was another half an hour before he finally flipped back the tarpaulin. The sky behind him had become charcoal grey with smudges of orange.

'I think it is dark enough for you to sit up now.'

'Thanks, Manolis,' said Callie. She was shivering all over.

'Do you know who that was in the motorboat?' Manolis asked, after he had wrapped them both in some dry canvas and given them hot coffee from his flask.

'He works for Skatelios,' said Callie.

'No, you are wrong,' Manolis contradicted her. 'He *is* Skatelios.

Nick almost fell out of the boat. 'Skatelios!'

'Andreas Skatelios – Georgiou Skatelios's son.'

'Was he around our dad's age?' asked Callie. 'And dressed in a suit?'

'That is him,' nodded Manolis. 'Though he did not look quite as smart as usual.'

'That'd be the fortress wall we dropped on him,' grinned Nick.

'But Skatelios was really brutal with him,' said Callie. 'He knocked him flying because he couldn't find us. His own son!'

'I have heard there is no love lost between father and son,' said Manolis.

Callie raised an eyebrow. It looked like Andreas was in for a very bad night when he went home empty-handed.

Manolis couldn't stand the suspense any longer. 'Callie, why is Georgiou Skatelios chasing you? What have you done? And where are your mother and father?'

Callie sighed. It was becoming a very long story. With Nick's help, she told Manolis everything that had happened, even how they had hidden King Akanon's map in the vineyard. By the time they finished the story, Manolis had a boat full of brown lobsters, and had sailed back down the coast. He was steering into the small harbour where his dad's taverna was. Coloured lights were twinkling, marking out the position of The Grapes taverna, while other lights speckled the hillside where people lived. The moon was white and almost a full circle above the sea.

Manolis ran a hand through his dark hair. 'What will you do now?'

Callie shrugged. She hadn't had time to think about it. 'We still have the clay tablets. Skatelios won't harm our parents while we have those.'

'And when he gets them he'll kill us all,' said Nick quietly.

Callie swallowed a lump in her throat. 'You can't tell your mum and dad, Manolis. We've already put *you* in danger. I'm not going to get *them* into trouble as well,' she said.

Manolis thought for a moment. 'We have an outhouse behind the taverna. It's rarely used and you would be safe there tonight without my father ever knowing.'

Callie nodded. She was much too tired to find somewhere else.

Manolis tied his boat to a mooring ring underneath the harbour wall and helped Callie climb up the stone steps. 'This way.' He led them away from the taverna at first, further along the pebbled beach and up a winding footpath used by people from the village. Then he doubled back behind a lemon grove and through a gap in his garden wall. Callie could smell fragrant jasmine and hear the screech of crickets.

The outhouse was far better than she could ever have hoped for. For a start, it actually had beds! And a little washstand and a tiny toilet. Right now it was even better than the Hotel Thelta.

'We use the outhouse when our guest rooms are full, but this week we have two empty rooms in the taverna,' explained Manolis. 'Do not turn the lights on though,' he warned them. 'They can be seen from my parents' bedroom.'

Nick half climbed, half fell onto the nearest bed. 'Night night,' he mumbled, and closed his eyes.

Manolis laughed, 'Night night, Niko.'

Callie smiled and gave him a weak hug, before she collapsed onto the other bed. She was fast asleep before Manolis even closed the door.

10
A GOLDEN PROPOSITION

Callie was dreaming...

King Akanon's ship, The Lion, *was ploughing across the Aegean Sea with countless other ships. Its wooden hull was elongated and sleek, and its prow stood high in the water, the bow curved on either side to slice through the waves. The oblong sail, with the lion's head embroidered upon it in red and gold, was stretched to every stitch and seam, capturing the wind and blasting the ship forward. Akanon's warriors were pushing the speed higher still with mighty oars punching through the water.*

Callie saw that Akanon was forward, the onward rush of air streaming through his golden hair. He looked fearless. What army in all the world could withstand a thousand ships, the might and power of Greece?

'Nestor.' Akanon summoned one of his royal guards. Nestor moved to his side, holding a page-sized wooden tray filled with damp clay, and a stylus for writing on it. 'Write down these words, good Nestor, and despatch them on the ship bound for home tomorrow.'

'Yes, my King.'

'My sister,' King Akanon began. 'Soon we shall sight the Trojan shore and I would make good my promise...'

Nestor was scratching lines and marks swiftly into the clay.

King Akanon went on. 'I would guide you now to the map. These are the four locations: secret names that no other shall know... The first—'

Callie felt herself drifting away, still being rocked gently by the waves, but falling far behind the Greek fleet. Far behind. The lion sail was shrinking into the distance... And the ship carrying King Akanon's message must never have reached Thelta.

Callie was awoken suddenly and startlingly by the door crashing open.

She jerked her body off the bed from the position she'd slept in all night. Nick fell right off his bed.

'The police are coming here. Now!' It was Manolis, speaking urgently.

'How? How could they have found us?' Callie stammered.

'My father – he has called them.'

Callie stopped. 'Why?'

'He saw the bathroom light on.'

Callie shot a glance at Nick, who pulled a guilty expression. 'Whoops.'

'He did not know that it was you and Niko.'

'Don't worry,' said Callie. 'We'll be all right and we'll try to let you know we're safe.'

'If you need me, signal me.' Manolis produced a sturdy-looking torch. 'I check the lobster pots at dawn and at dusk. I have brought this also...' Manolis handed Callie a pink backpack, virtually the same as the one she'd lost at the fortress. 'Left here by a tourist last summer.'

Callie snatched up their things from the floor, including the plastic bag containing their money and phones and stuffed them all into the backpack. 'Thanks, Manolis.'

'Now go!'

A misty, apricot-tinted dawn had settled across the sea as Callie led the way. She slipped quickly through the gap in the garden wall and retraced the circuitous route Manolis had taken them the night before. The footpath would lead them away from the Mount Thelta road, the road the police would come on, and back to the pebble beach.

After five minutes of walking they still hadn't heard either police sirens, or a car engine. Maybe the police had decided not to bother. Callie started to breathe again.

It was too soon to let down her guard. Smartly Dressed Man – Andreas Skatelios, had stepped out right in front of her. He looked dishevelled, as if he had spent the night on the beach.

Callie thought he was about to make a grab for her. Instead, he said, 'You must listen to me. I can restore your parents to you.'

'Come on!' shouted Nick, dragging Callie into a run.

Andreas thundered after them. 'I despise my father. I am not part of his insane plans,' he shouted at their backs.

Callie risked a look over her shoulder to see how far behind he was. It was a mistake. A tree root sticking out from the ground sent her sprawling into the bushes at the edge of the beach. Andreas was upon her before she even worked out what had happened. Unexpectedly, he helped her up and then stepped back, making no attempt to restrain her.

Nick skidded to a halt and raced back.

'I will not stop you escaping,' Andreas said firmly. 'But I *can* save your parents.'

Callie stared at him. He looked very like his father: tall and strong, only younger and without the same white hair and the hatred in his eyes.

'How did you find us?' she demanded.

'I followed the red and yellow boat in the darkness.'

Callie recoiled. Andreas knew that Manolis had helped them. 'How did you know we were on it?'

'I saw you move the tarpaulin... Lobsters do not have pink fingers.'

Callie looked down the track, judging how far they could get before he caught them again. Andreas seemed to guess what she was thinking.

'Go now if you cannot trust me. I will not stop you.'

'How can you save our parents?' Nick demanded.

'My father has them on Skatelios Island.' He waved vaguely in the direction of the sea. Skatelios Island was a vague dot on the misty horizon. 'He needs their expertise. They have seen the map and can lead him to the keys. I can spirit them away from the island.'

Callie was still staring at him. She couldn't think of a single reason why she should believe him.

'I have friends who can get your family away from Thelta.'

'What's in it for you?' Nick asked bluntly.

'You have seen how my father treats me, but I cannot escape him without money. King Akanon's gold is a great deal of money.'

Callie frowned. 'You want the map?'

'No. My father would suspect me if I began searching all over the island for keys. You must retrieve the keys and open the treasury *for me*, then I will deliver your parents...'

'But how can we?' stammered Callie. *'We're kids.'*

'Find a way.'

After a long pause, Callie nodded. 'How can we get in touch with you?'

Andreas gave her his mobile phone number.

'How can we trust *him* any more than we can trust his dad?' Nick wanted to know.

They had found the track to Thelta Town, and it had brought them right back to the vineyard where they'd buried the map.

'I don't think he's got the stomach for killing,' replied Callie. 'He could have taken us when we were on Manolis's boat but he didn't. And he didn't look very hard for us when we were on the scaffolding outside the fortress, either, did he?'

'Bet he wished he had after, though,' grinned Nick.

Callie squinted at the horizon in case it was all a trick and Andreas was following them. 'I think it's safe,' she finally concluded. The only person they'd seen since

Andreas was a farmer loading baskets of watermelons onto a donkey. That had been nearly an hour ago.

'Ten, eight,' Nick reminded her.

Callie smiled. If nothing else, she'd taught her brother when her birthday was. She let him count out the paces and start digging.

'If King Akanon's Treasury is right under our villa,' he said after a few minutes' work, 'why can't we just blast our way through with some explosives or a bulldozer or something?'

'Erm – a, we don't have any explosives. And b, we don't have a bulldozer.' Nick pulled a face. 'Anyway, if you don't use the keys, the ceiling is booby-trapped to collapse and bury all the treasure, and anyone in there with it.'

'How do you know that?'

'Part of the legend. It's in all the books Mum and Dad wrote.'

Nick stopped digging. 'Do you really think they're all right? Mum and Dad?'

Callie nodded. 'You heard what Andreas said. Without the map, Skatelios needs them.'

'I suppose.'

Nick's stick scraped against something hard and he began lifting the clay tablets out of the soil, one by one. Callie peered over the wall to check there was still no one about. She didn't like being out here in the open at all.

'Well, that was the easy bit,' said Nick. 'Now what do we do?'

'Find somewhere safe, and read the map.'

Most of the people staying at Hotel Thelta had either gone out to lie on the beach or were heading off on day trips. Only a few hadn't made it further than the hotel swimming pool. Callie and Nick were sitting with them, at a white plastic table, and Callie was assembling King Akanon's map.

Nick gaped at her. 'Won't people wonder why two kids have got a three-thousand-year-old map? *The* three-thousand-year-old map!'

'They'll just think it's a ten euro souvenir if you stop drawing attention to it!'

'But it's different. It's completely different,' said Nick.

Callie stared at the completed map. 'Only if you look closely at it. Whoever made the souvenir actually did quite a good job. They must have worked out how big the whole puzzle was from the piece in the archaeological museum.'

'The piece that Dad stole.'

'Dad didn't steal it,' Callie corrected him.

'I suppose it's more interesting than being an archaeologist,' shrugged Nick.

'What is?'

'Being a thief.'

'He's not a thief!'

One of the hotel guests, a fat man wearing a T-shirt and shorts and sporting a frightening suntan, the same bright red colour as a cooked lobster, had stopped to admire

118

King Akanon's map.

'Have you found the treasure yet?' he asked, in a cultured, English accent.

Nick nearly leapt into the swimming pool. He hadn't seen the hotel guest standing right behind him.

'No, we've only just started,' said Callie sweetly, leaning her arm across the map to cover it.

'Mine has "Welcome To Thelta" on it.'

'We had one of those first but Callie broke it,' said Nick, recovering slightly.

'I think it's just a gimmick, to bring tourists to the island,' the hotel guest went on.

Nick looked the man up and down. 'That, and sunbathing.' Callie kicked him under the table.

'Well, happy hunting,' smiled the hotel guest.

'See,' Callie said, watching him head out through the door, 'Lobster Tan Man thought it was a souvenir.' But her breathing was extremely uneven.

Now she was able to study the map properly, she could see that it was very detailed. The entire surface was covered in markings and symbols, and an upside-down 'Y' shape on the middle section pointed to all three corners of the island.

Most of the markings were small pictures like on any modern map, though what they represented on *this* map, Callie could only guess at. There were many boat-like symbols around the edges. As they didn't appear anywhere inland, Callie assumed they meant 'harbour' or 'port'. Lots of squares all bunched together had to mean a town or a city, and three straight vertical lines together might represent a temple. Then Callie counted at least thirty other types of symbol which were a complete mystery to her. Worse still, the unreadable symbols were thickest at the three corners of Thelta. Right where they would need to look, it was least clear. And, after some three thousand years, what, if anything, was left of King Akanon's Thelta? How were they ever going to solve this?

'Well?'

Callie stared at her brother. 'Well what?'

'Where are the keys?'

Callie snorted. 'It's not that easy!' She pointed at the map. 'The middle piece is like a key itself. That's why Dad needed it. Look.'

She showed Nick the three-pointed symbol like an upside-down letter 'Y' in the centre of the completed map. 'That's the direction, and here's where you measure from.'

'Where? Where's here?'

'It's Mount Thelta. And if you were measuring from a mountain, you'd measure from the highest point, and that's on the modern map!' She took out a detailed road map of Thelta which they'd bought on their way to the hotel.

'So – measure.'

'It's in Mycenaean feet.'

'Oh. Mycenaean feet,' said Nick, trying to sound knowledgeable.

Callie knew very well that he had no idea what a

Mycenaean foot was. 'It's like nought point nine-o-one recurring of our feet. But modern maps are marked in kilometres and metres, so we need to convert it.'

'There's got to be a way,' said Nick.

'There is a way, but we're going to need a computer.'

Nick thought for a moment. 'What about that internet café?'

'What internet café?'

'In the town.'

Callie couldn't remember seeing an internet café. 'Are you sure?'

'Yep. Dad sent some emails from there the other day.'

Callie started taking the map to pieces again. 'Okay then. Show me.'

11

THELTANTREASURE.COM

It was situated uncomfortably close to Thelta Town police station, and was a Greek-style internet café. They really did serve coffee in tiny little cups, and the coffee was thick and sticky and barely diluted at all!

The internet café owner was tall and dapper with a neatly trimmed moustache and slicked back hair. He was a one-man King Akanon's Treasury, wearing an expensive gold wristwatch, several gold rings, and displaying at least one gold tooth right at the front of his mouth. They paid him three euros and got to work.

The computers were quite grubby, particularly the keyboards. Otherwise they were no worse than the ones at Callie's school. They had standard keyboards with familiar layout and lettering, except some of the letters had the Greek variant printed underneath.

Callie tapped in a website she'd seen her dad use. It had every modern and ancient measurement listed, from fathoms to centimetres, inches to cubits. It even had a neat little conversion window where one unit of measurement could be typed in and, at the click of a mouse, converted into any other unit of measurement from the list. Callie found the length of a Mycenaean foot was 0.9102657 of a modern foot, and converted it into metres and kilometres. She printed off the results:

7.346748463km north. 7.3684648489km south-west. 7.2989875562km south-east.

'Easy when you know how,' she told Nick.

She typed in another website her dad used. An online route-finder opened on the computer screen. She entered the word 'Thelta', and the screen changed to a detailed and accurate map of the island.

The internet café owner wandered past, glancing at the computer screen with interest. When he'd gone, Callie moused over the map and clicked on the summit of Mount Thelta. Then she selected a 'distance' tool.

A pop-up appeared – a distance gauge which increased or decreased according to the position of the mouse pointer over the map. A small dial indicated the three-hundred and sixty degrees of the compass and was also controlled by the mouse.

When the direction lined up with north and the gauge read: 7.346748463km, Callie marked the position and printed out the entire section of the map. She started again, lining up south-west with 7.3684648489km, marking and printing it. Finally she input the third coordinate: 7.298987562km south-east, and printed out the map.

She picked up the coloured printouts from the printer tray and peered at them. Ominously, all three coordinates pointed to absolutely nothing, unless you counted the sea.

Nick was looking over her shoulder. 'There's nothing there.'

Callie sighed. 'I'll do it again.' She backed up on the

computer to the 'measurement wizard' and re-entered everything. Then she plotted the results on the map of Thelta once more.

'Is it different?' asked Nick, five minutes later.

'No. It's exactly the same.'

Callie tried to think. This couldn't be right. Okay, so most of the Thelta that King Akanon would have known had been destroyed by earthquakes, or had made room for modern Thelta, but there was still plenty of evidence of the Mycenaean period even today. There were remains of tombs, temples and palaces, and *they* were marked on the modern map.

Perhaps it was the distance? Was it really possible to convert an ancient measurement into a modern one?

Callie pressed the '+' key on the computer to zoom to the area of the map intersected by the line marking north. 'Maybe there's something on the line but not at those exact coordinates.'

There was: a hospital, a school and at least three vineyards. 'Unless they were as desperate as us, they won't have buried keys in vineyards,' sighed Callie.

'And not in a school or hospital either,' said Nick. He was chewing his fingernails nervously.

The line going in a south-westerly direction only seemed to produce hotels and a football ground. And the south-easterly line intersected with a massive amount of modern day Thelta, but not a single feature which looked as if it might be old.

'It must be something else,' groaned Callie, massaging her aching forehead.

Nick sighed. 'Unless north used to be in a different place.'

Callie stared at him, a look of realisation on her face.

'That's it! North *did* used to be in a different place!'

'What?' Nick gaped at her as if she'd gone completely mad.

'Dad wrote about it in one of his books!'

'Did he... ?'

'It's called precession or something like that. It's to do with the earth wobbling on its axis over thousands of years and making north change slightly. It's over three-thousand years since the map was made, and if the compass was different by just one or two degrees, the lines could go straight past what we're looking for.'

Nick flopped back in his chair. 'Then we've got no chance.'

Callie hadn't given up. 'Pass me those maps.'

Nick handed her the three printouts and she studied them again. One centimetre to the left of the spot marked on the northern corner of Thelta it said: *palace (remains of)*. The compass *had* been different! She shuffled the printouts and looked one centimetre to the left of the point marked on the map of the south-east. Again, she found something instantly: the words *ancient theatre*. One centimetre to the left of the coordinates on the third map was a name: *Nekrotafio*.

'What's a Nekrotafio?' asked Nick.

Callie shook her head. 'I don't know. It could be the name of the place. We won't know until we get there.' Callie felt more relieved than she could ever remember. They could do this after all.

Nick pointed at the computer screen. 'Have you done?'

'I suppose so. Why?'

Nick reached for the off button and pressed it. All the data that Callie had input was instantly lost. Nobody else would be able to access it. 'A little trick I learned at home,' Nick explained.

'No wonder Dad's always losing stuff off his computer.'

They paid another two euros for the printing, and headed for the door.

'So which of these places do we go to first?' asked Nick.

'I don't think it matters. So probably the nearest.'

Around the corner from the internet café, Callie stopped to buy lunch from a stall. She bought two massive sausage rolls with flaky pastry. The meat tasted *different* but very good. They sat on a bench eating them.

'Did you see that?' asked Nick, with his mouth full.

'What?'

'That woman with the shopping basket. She turned right round to stare at us, and then she told her friend to look as well.'

Callie followed Nick's gaze. 'It's not like Greek people to stare at you. They're usually so polite.'

'Let's go somewhere else.'

The moment they stood up, Callie realised why the woman with the basket was staring at them. On a lamppost at the side of the street was a poster with their photos on it. The Greek writing probably said: MISSING KIDS, CONTACT POLICE.

'Oh no! Khrisous! It's got to be,' said Callie, out of the corner of her mouth. 'No wonder she's looking at us.'

'That's really gonna make things difficult,' said Nick. He started to peel the poster off the lamppost.

'It's no good doing that,' hissed Callie. 'There's bound to be more, and you'll never get rid of them all.'

'I'm not trying to get rid of it. I want it as a souvenir.'

Nick carefully folded up the poster and put it into his pocket.

The woman with the shopping basket had spotted a policeman in grey and blue uniform, stopping lunch time traffic to ease a large lorry through the narrow street. She went running over to him, and grabbed him by the arm. Then she pointed straight at Callie and Nick and started gabbling at him.

The policeman tried shaking the woman off, but she was having none of it and dragged him to a second lamppost displaying another poster. Finally he understood. Callie realised she was still watching as the policeman spoke into the walkie-talkie clipped to his breast pocket.

'Callie, come on!' Nick shouted.

Callie and the policeman started to run at the same moment. There were fewer than thirty metres between them.

Nick was in front, and Callie chased after him. He dived straight into an open-air fruit market, busy with shoppers picking out the ripest, juiciest fruits. Nick dodged around them deftly and ran to what looked like a dead end where two stalls made a corner. It was part of his plan, because after a quick glance back at Callie, he dropped to his knees and rolled right underneath a table displaying watermelons, and out through a canvas flap at the back of the market.

Callie copied the manoeuvre, leaving the policeman sprawling amongst rolling watermelons and being shouted at by incensed stallholders.

As Callie rolled out behind the market, Nick was already running along the harbour wall. She sprinted after him. The policeman burst out of the market and continued to chase her down.

With dismay, Callie realised they were running out of harbour wall! To the left was the back of a large warehouse, to the right the water and straight ahead a gap where boats could load and unload. They were trapped!

Nick barely paused, running straight up a wooden gangplank and onto the deck of a yacht with a luxury cabin and a towering mast. In five paces he'd made it across the deck and was clambering up onto the harbour wall on the far side. Callie scrambled after him. The captain of the yacht ran out of his cabin and started screaming at her in angry Greek.

Nick waited only a moment for Callie, before turning aside to the busy road which ran right the way along Thelta Town's seafront. He aimed for a gap in the traffic, making car horns sound angrily. There was a squeal of tyre rubber and a white car with a navy stripe skidded to a halt to cut him off. The front passenger door was already flying open.

'Khrisous!' The policeman must have radioed Khrisous to tell him where they were. Nick swerved out of his reach and onto the other side of the carriageway, straight in front of a coach. The coach driver stood on his brakes, making his coach skid to a stop. Callie sped past both Khrisous and coach, and caught up with Nick on the pavement.

There was a taverna in front of them, with tables spilling out onto the pavement. Greek people were lounging in cane furniture drinking coffee. Callie and Nick dashed through them, upsetting a couple of empty chairs and ran into the taverna. There was a long wooden serving bar at right angles to the street. Callie and Nick raced straight down the length of it to an open doorway at the back of the taverna.

At the last minute, Callie dragged Nick back behind a massive stack of Greek Cola cans in packs of six, wrapped in see-through plastic. She put a finger to her lips warningly and squatted down out of sight.

Khrisous and the policeman came clattering through the taverna and straight out the back door. Callie held her palm up to caution Nick to stay put. A moment later they heard Khrisous and the policeman coming back inside. Khrisous was yelling maniacally in Greek. Callie guessed exactly what he was saying: 'Don't let them get out of this town! I want to kill them with my bare hands!'

12
LOBSTER TAN MAN

'What about that one?' Nick was pointing at the latest arrival, a sleek yellow and white coach with *FarTours* written down its side in blue lettering.

They'd found the area of the waterfront where excursion coaches picked up and dropped off. They had to get out of Thelta Town before anyone else recognised them from the posters.

'It looks almost full,' said Callie. 'Let's wait for one with a few more empty seats.'

They were going to slip out of Thelta Town among a coachload of English tourists. All they had to do was find a coach with some empty seats on, and walk back on board with the day-trippers. First though they had to wait for the right coach to arrive and unload, to make sure it *had* empty seats. Callie was relying on the fact that when anyone had been sitting on a bus, and got back on again, they always seemed to return to the same seats. If a coach had empty seats she and Nick could take them without anyone even noticing. 'We'll get caught straight away if someone accuses us of taking their seats.'

Maybe the coach might even stop near one of the places they'd marked on the map.

'This one looks better,' decided Callie as a white coach with red stripes belonging to *Island Express* pulled in.

She could see three sets of empty seats along the left-hand side of the coach. She counted along. The first empty seats were nine rows back. 'We need to listen at the door.'

They wandered to the front of the coach where everybody was piling off. The passengers were speaking English, and the Greek coach driver was giving them their departure time. 'Ladies and gentlemen, we leave at two fifty-five... Two fifty-five please, ladies and gentlemen,' he kept repeating, as more and more people climbed off.

Two fifty-five. That was another hour away. They'd have to wait and go on board when everybody started returning.

They used the time to buy baseball caps and sunglasses from a souvenir stall, in an attempt to disguise themselves. Then they bought some more sausage rolls and a bottle of water.

When they returned, the coach had moved to the front of the bus queue, and people were starting to climb back on.

Callie's heart was pounding somewhere around her throat. She was suddenly terrified. They were never going to get away with this!

Nick was looking at her to take the lead. She took a deep breath and attached herself to a couple of adults around her parents' age, yanking Nick along with her. 'I'm bored! And it's so hot! Can't we just go to the beach?' she started, spouting a list of complaints. 'I'm really tired!'

The couple ignored her, just like her own parents would have done, and suddenly all four of them were past the coach driver. Callie counted back nine rows on the left-hand side of the coach and then slipped into the seat by the window. Nick sat down beside her. 'That was brilliant!' he whispered.

'Thanks.'

The coach was filling up and the seats around them were soon claimed. Conversations were about what everyone had seen in Thelta Town: the shopping *palatia*, the markets, the waterfront cafés, and about where they were stopping next.

'Villastoli!' Callie recognised the name. There was a monastery there, high up in the hills. She consulted the maps she'd printed off, and, Yes! The *palace (remains of)* was barely a kilometre from the Villastoli Monastery.

'We're going in the right direction.' She blew out her cheeks and allowed herself to relax.

'Where do you think you two are going?'

Callie's heart stopped. The last person to board the coach was standing right in front of them.

'Erm... We were... Er...' Callie stammered.

Other passengers were starting to turn and stare.

'You shouldn't be on here.'

Callie thought she was going to die.

'You'll never find King Akanon's treasure if you spend all your time sightseeing.'

Callie blinked and suddenly recognised him. It was the

man with the lobster red suntan who'd spoken to them at the hotel. She managed to find her voice again and with a stroke of inspiration said: 'Tell Mum and Dad that. The last thing we want to do is visit some STUPID MONASTERY!' She directed her words at the couple they'd boarded the coach with, and glared at the back of their heads.

Lobster Tan looked embarrassed by Callie's teenage tantrum, and hurried off to claim his own seat further down the coach.

'Well done, sis,' croaked Nick, sounding as if he was going to be sick. Callie found she was shaking all over.

The last passengers to take their seats were a family who seemed to have bought every souvenir in Thelta Town, including two inflatable turtles. As they stowed their souvenirs the driver took a cursory head count, and decided he had 'at least' as many passengers as before. He operated the coach doors with a final-sounding 'shwoosh'.

Callie started nibbling her fingernails. They had just cornered themselves, and now there would be no escape until the coach stopped at Villastoli.

They were soon moving through traffic. The coach drove first along the waterfront, past both the market and the police station, and after a last view of the glittering sea, rumbled through the suburbs to a road which wound slowly into the foothills. The road hugged a pine-forested hillside, overhanging a hideous drop. The whole coach felt as if it was going to swing right out over the edge as the driver negotiated each twist and turn.

Callie's heart was in her mouth as a truck overtook them, reminding her of the scarlet red truck which had tried to force their jeep off the road only two days ago. She decided not to look out of the window any more.

Nick had recovered sufficiently to look at the poster they'd found in Thelta Town.

'Stop waving that about,' Callie implored.

'I'm going to get it framed and put on my bedroom wall,' Nick announced. He tucked it away again and asked, 'Do you really think we're going to find the keys...? I mean, they're not going to be lying under a plant pot, are they, else someone'd've already found them.'

Callie had been thinking the same thing. 'It's obviously going to be difficult.' Nick stared at her. 'What are you looking at me like that for?'

'I thought you were going to say – Don't worry, it's going to be really easy.'

'Sorry.'

Callie tried to make them both feel better by adding: 'There's more clues on the clay tablets though, but we can't work them out until we get to each place and see what's around...Anyway, I'm going to get some sleep. Wake me up when we get to the monastery.'

She leaned her head between the headrest and the coach window and closed her eyes.

BANG! There was a shuddering blow as the two Greek ships collided, shattering hull timbers, and buckling decks.

134

For a minute they were locked together before the storm separated them – the side of one was torn away and the other lost its mast.

Callie saw King Akanon regain his feet and climb over the splintered deck as the wind and rain lashed his face like a barbed whip. Great spurts of water were pumping into his ship from the waves. The Lion *would sink in minutes.*

Akanon was looking for the rest of the Greek fleet through the curtain of rain, but only The Sea Serpent, *the ship they had just been smashed against, was visible. He strained his eyes against the blinding rain.* The Sea Serpent *was wallowing and dragging its mast but was still soundly afloat.*

'She is whole. We must transfer to The Serpent,' *Akanon cried. 'Hurry, we have only moments.'*

Callie saw it at the same instant as Akanon – a mountainous wave that would drive the two ships back together, or act as a wedge, forcing them further apart. If it were the latter, King Akanon and the forty greatest warriors in all of Thelta would be lost to the ocean.

'Turn her into the face of the storm,' yelled King Akanon, his strong voice belying his youth. 'We must throw her into the path of the wave.'

He dragged Nestor, his royal guard, to the nearest oar and made him dig it deep into the water. Nestor understood instantly, as did the rest of the crew, who put muscle to wood.

At first, The Lion *was unresponsive, dead in the water. Then, at the last minute, the shifting water filling her hull* tipped her to one side and the oars dipped deep enough to turn it into the wave. The rushing wall of sea slammed into her like a battering ram, and the noise was thunderous. The whole deck slanted beneath King Akanon, and the ship was carried inexorably towards help.

Callie watched as Neptolomus, the captain of The Sea Serpent and a commander of the Second Theltan chariot squadron, saw The Lion bearing down on his ship for a second collision. He abandoned his attempts to cut free the trailing mast and roared at his men to brace for impact.

King Akanon hailed him as the two ships closed. 'Neptolomus! You must take us aboard. We are done for.' The words were snatched from King Akanon's lips by the howling gale, but Neptolomus could see The Lion would sink and was already shouting orders to his crew.

As the ships came together with a mighty crash. King Akanon was driving those taller and older than himself forward. 'Go. GO! I command you!' They scrambled across to The Sea Serpent, and turned to find King Akanon was not among them.

The angry sea was ripping through the planks of The Lion. More than half of her was underwater.

'Akanon – jump!' Neptolomus was screaming at his king.

'You have no steering! I must push The Lion away or she'll take The Serpent with her.'

'But my King…'

Akanon flashed a boyish grin. 'As soon as she clears I'll jump. Be ready to fish me from the sea, Great Neptolomus.' He snatched up a wooden spar, twice as long as himself, and

136

jammed it against the other vessel. Slowly, the ships began to separate. When it was enough, King Akanon climbed the starboard rail, and leapt... It was at that moment the storm battered the remains of The Lion *in the stern, and tossed it a full twenty lengths from its former position. Both crews crowded the rails of Neptolomus's ship.* The Lion *was gone, and King Akanon with it.*

Nick was shaking Callie awake. 'We're here.'

'Wha...Oh!'

The monastery at Villastoli was halfway up a mountain, and for the last part of the journey was reached via a long series of zigzagging stone steps, under the shelter of tamarisk trees with feathery clusters of pink blooms.

The *Island Express* was parked at the bottom of the steps, and the driver was cheerfully announcing that they had an hour to walk all the way to the top, look round and then walk all the way back down again. 'Sixty minutes please, ladies and gentlemen. Sixty minutes...'

As everyone spilled from the coach and started the climb, Callie dawdled and stopped Nick from racing ahead.

'We need to hang back so we can turn off on our own without being noticed,' she whispered. 'We don't want half the coach following us!'

'I don't know,' said Nick. 'They might come in handy if we run into Skatelios.'

'That's not funny.'

They sauntered along with the stragglers who were finding the climb taxing in the hot sun, until several people gave up and started back down. Lobster Tan Man was among them.

'I've decided I don't want to see the monastery after all,' he panted, as he lumbered past.

'Gone to work on his tan more like,' said Nick.

Now they had a whole section of stone steps to themselves. At intervals the trees opened out to afford a glimpse of the monastery. The walls were built of the same yellow-coloured rock it was perched on. It was a set of domed towers clustered together like a collection of giant salt cellars, except the domes were constructed of curved terracotta tiles, and the towers were punctured by intricate arches made of stone and brick.

Callie checked the map. 'We need to go almost to the top and then see if we can find a footpath heading off to the north.'

'We ought to get a move on,' said Nick. 'We don't want to be still going up when everyone else starts coming back down again.'

They picked up their pace. Nick used it as an excuse to charge off but was soon flagging, and Callie easily overtook him. 'I thought you were in a hurry,' she grinned.

Nick pulled a face.

They found the footpath overgrown and untended, as if the palace remains were far less of a local attraction than the monastery. Callie supposed that if you only had an hour to get back to the coach, you could hardly visit both. They turned aside.

Although it was less steep on the footpath than the steps, the thick vegetation made it no less difficult. They seemed to be walking for ages before the path finally opened out onto a wide, flat ledge cut into the side of the hill, and overlooking the horseshoe-shaped bay of Villastoli. It was an incredible view. No wonder King Akanon had built one of his palaces up here.

Callie could see the main road zigzagging its way up from Thelta Town, and on it a white and red coach, heading down.

'Well, we've missed the bus,' said Nick cheerfully.

It must have taken them more than an hour to get here! Callie hadn't imagined they'd get back in time anyway.

The words *palace (remains of)* written on the modern map were certainly accurate. All that was left of the palace was the layout. It had once been a *megaron* – a Mycenaean great hall, with apartments and storerooms leading off it. Foundation stones, a large paved area, a few overgrown steps and hopefully, a priceless key, were all that remained.

'Not much left, is there?' said Nick.

Callie swallowed a lump in her throat. How on earth could one of King Akanon's keys still be hidden *here*? She sat down on one of the steps and opened her backpack. She shared out more Theltan-style sausage rolls and water with Nick, and found the clay tablet relating to the palace remains. She rested her chin on the palm of her hand and studied the tiny markings in the clay.

There looked to be an 'O' and an 'H.' What did that mean? Had it some meaning in Mycenaean? Maybe the word 'OH' had been engraved on one of the buildings. If that was it, they had NO chance of finding it. There was nothing left standing higher than a few centimetres.

Nick glanced at the clay tablet while he was stuffing his face with sausage roll.

'Where's the clue?'

'There, where it says "OH".' Callie pointed to the word.

Nick peered at the clay tablet with a thoughtful expression. 'We have to find the well and climb down.'

'What well? What are you on about?'

Nick was shaking his head. 'It's not "OH", it's a circle and a ladder. The circle means there's a well, and the ladder means we've got to climb down it.'

Callie stared at the clay tablet again. What she had taken for an 'H', had indeed got two close rungs across it like a ladder. She let out a little laugh.

'See! There *is* a point to playing computer games,' said Nick.

Callie carefully folded the piece of the map into some tissues and returned it to her backpack. She took a couple of bites of her sausage roll and then said: 'Okay, brainiac, where's the well?'

It wasn't hard to find. There was a ring of kerbstones around a narrow shaft sunk into the earth.

Nick dropped a lump of wall rubble into it and they both listened. They didn't even hear it land. Callie got out Manolis's torch and shone it down. The inside was a perfect circle of stonework as far down as the torch beam reached. There was one small problem – if you were meant to climb down there, there was no ladder. If it was any consolation, the key was probably still hidden, because there was no way of getting to it.

'I don't suppose you've got any rope ladders in there?' said Nick, pointing at Callie's backpack.

'Right out of them.'

Callie sighed and looked up into the sky. The sun was almost overhead but there still wasn't enough brightness to shine all the way to the bottom of the well. The inside was pitted in places, though not nearly enough to provide hand or footholds, and there were no gaps between the blocks. She'd learned to abseil last winter on an outward bound course in Wales, and she'd also tried a climbing wall – a specially built wall with different-coloured blocks pegged into it to grip or stand on. But this was un-climbable. Even a really experienced climber wouldn't attempt it. It was just impossible.

Callie handed her backpack to Nick and swung her legs over the edge of the well.

'You must be joking!' Nick exclaimed.

'We don't have any choice, do we?'

'Please, Callie! Don't!'

'Look, I wouldn't try it if I didn't think I could do it.'

She took a firm grip of the kerbstone and lowered her body into the well shaft. She felt around with her feet until she found a small toehold, and then started feeling for somewhere else to grip with her fingers. Unexpectedly, her hand was swallowed up by one of the pitted areas. It was far deeper than it had looked from above, and inside was an iron bar, a hand's width wide. Callie gripped it gratefully and transferred her weight to feel for another foothold further down.

There was a grating sound. Her weight was too much for the iron bar and it had started to move. She was pulling it right out of the wall. Callie screamed.

13
THE FIRST KEY

All she was holding on to was a moving iron bar!

With a click, the iron bar stopped. Callie let out a gasp of relief.

'What happened?' Nick called down, waving the torch.

'I don't know. Aim the torch down to where I've got my hand.'

Nick redirected the torchlight onto the wall. From inside the well she could see a vague stain on the wall, like a charcoal birthmark and in the shape of a lion's head. There was a hole, right where the lion's mouth should be, and inside the mouth was a small iron handle which pulled out.

'I've found the ladder.'

She could now see another identical lion birthmark around thirty centimetres below the first. She felt inside its open mouth for a second handle. This time she pulled it out to a stop before transferring her weight. Twenty more handles and Callie had become an expert at using the lion ladder. She kept going, losing count of the rungs and feeling exhilarated. Only somebody in total desperation would have tried to climb down, and that made her convinced the key would still be hidden where it had been placed more than three thousand years ago.

'Are you at the bottom yet?' Nick's voice sounded miles away.

'No. It just keeps going on and on,' Callie shouted back, making her ears hurt with the echo. She continued descending, starting to tire.

The next rung felt immediately different. The bar was thicker, and, instead of sliding to a stop, it came right out of the wall. Suddenly she was no longer climbing – she was falling.

She hit the floor of the well with a thud. It was only a metre below her but she would have preferred not to land on it bottom-first. She couldn't see a thing, yet she was smiling all over her face. She knew that what she had in her hand was a large key. They were one third of the way to opening King Akanon's Treasury.

'I've got it!' she yelled up to Nick.

There was no answer. He must have got bored and wandered off. She buttoned the key safely into her pocket and started the long climb back up.

Halfway to the top, she stopped to rest. 'Nick...?' If he'd eaten all the food she was going to kill him. She started again, aiming for the circle of light. After five more minutes she pulled herself out over the kerbstone.

'Thank you. I don't think I could have made that climb myself.'

It was the third time Callie had heard that voice today. It was Lobster Tan Man, and he was gripping Nick by the scruff of the neck. He must have doubled back just so he could follow them to the palace ruins.

'He threatened to throw rocks down on you if I tried to warn you,' spat Nick.

'But you're...' Callie began.

'A harmless tourist?'

Callie frowned. That was exactly what she had thought.

'Did you think Mr Skatelios only employed Greeks?' sneered Lobster Tan. 'And did you think he wouldn't have the hotels watched? For goodness sake, how many places on Thelta *could* two English children go *without* drawing attention to themselves? Now give me the key!'

'Let my brother go.'

Instead of letting Nick go, Lobster Tan forced him over to the edge of the well. He held him precariously over the opening. One small push, and—

'Maybe I should have said, give me the key or your brother here takes the short cut to the bottom.'

'Don't give him it,' said Nick angrily.

Callie took the bronze key from her pocket and threw it to Lobster Tan. He caught it deftly and shoved Nick at Callie, instead of down the well.

'Mr Skatelios will reward me handsomely for this,' he said. 'I'm hoping to buy my *own* Greek island when I have enough funds.'

He only glanced at the key, before taking out his mobile phone and dialling a number. Callie was staring at the key! It had a long bronze stem with a lion's head on one end of it. The other end looked very intricate, with around a dozen teeth, all of different lengths. The whole thing was twenty centimetres long.

Lobster Tan spoke into his mobile. 'James Spearman here. I have the key, and I have them...Good. At the bottom of the steps then in one hour.'

Callie was mouthing the word 'Run' to Nick. He nodded and they bolted off together.

'I said, I have them,' repeated Lobster Tan, this time for their benefit. A piece of rock shattered in front of Callie, and at the same instant she registered the sound of a gunshot. She stopped and looked back. Lobster Tan was aiming a pistol at her head.

'That wasn't a miss. That was a warning,' he informed her. 'Now come back here.'

Callie nodded to Nick. They had no other option.

Lobster Tan picked up Callie's backpack from the ground and rummaged through it until he found the clay tablets. 'You don't know how hard it was not to just take these from you at the hotel. Unfortunately there were too many witnesses.'

'So you followed us all morning,' guessed Callie.

'Nearly lost you when the police chased you,' admitted Lobster Tan. 'If I hadn't decided to check that café for myself I wouldn't have spotted you sneaking out the back.'

'You even got on the coach the same way we did,' said Callie.

'Yes, a rather good idea of yours. Still a little too public though.'

'Prefer to pick on kids when no one's about, do you?' Nick didn't even try to hide his contempt.

146

'As it happens, I did Mr Skatelios a favour by waiting. Now he won't have to decipher the map himself.' He was thumbing through the map printouts which Callie had taken off the computer. 'Who knows, it may have taken him weeks to work out.'

He stuffed everything back into the backpack, including the bronze key, and zipped it up.

'Here.' He thrust it at Callie's chest. 'You can make yourself useful by carrying this. And don't get any ideas.' He waved the gun threateningly. 'Mr Skatelios really doesn't need you two any more, does he?'

Callie shivered and pulled the straps of the backpack over her shoulders.

Lobster Tan pointed to the overgrown footpath at the edge of the ruins with his gun. 'Now, if you'd be so good as to lead the way.'

It was hard going, and Lobster Tan was soon struggling with the heat and the terrain. He made them stop twice so he could rest and wipe his sweating forehead with the bottom of his T-shirt. Callie tried not to look, because every time he did it he exposed a round pig belly matted with ugly black hairs. It was the grossest thing she'd seen all holiday.

'Wait!' Lobster Tan told them after fifteen minutes, 'And hand me that water from your bag.'

Callie slipped the backpack off her shoulders and handed Lobster Tan the bottle of mineral water. He took several long, noisy gulps from it.

'What about us?' demanded Callie. Lobster Tan slowly

turned the bottle upside down and poured the remaining water onto the ground.

'Git!' said Nick, under his breath.

'Less for you to carry,' explained Lobster Tan scornfully. 'Now, if you don't mind, we have people waiting for us.'

Skatelios presumably, thought Callie, and then: Mum and Dad might be with him. Yet even if they were, she had failed. Once Skatelios had the map he'd have no further use for any of them.

She realised they'd reached the stone steps leading to the monastery. There were voices right below them. At first Callie thought it must be Skatelios and probably Glass Eye, having lost patience waiting, coming up to get them. Then she realised the voices were distinctly non-Greek. They were English. It must be the next coachload of tourists visiting the monastery.

Lobster Tan looked suddenly concerned. He gestured at Callie and Nick to stand by the side of the steps, and allow the stream of tourists past. Then, reluctantly, he pocketed his gun before the first of them appeared through the trees.

There must have been close to forty day-trippers tramping tiredly up the steps. Some of them smiled at Callie and Nick, and exchanged pleasantries like, 'Is it much further?' And, 'Is there a tea room up there?'

Soon almost everyone was past. If Callie didn't make her move now it would be too late. 'I'll race you to the top!' she yelled at Nick, and sprang off before Lobster Tan could stop her. Nick must have been planning the same thing because he overtook her in just a few steps.

Callie's mind was racing along with her feet. Lobster Tan had to come after them. In his laziness, he'd made her carry the printouts, the clay tablets and the first key! Fear of being caught lent her speed. Nick was way ahead and they were both overtaking tourists one by one. Lobster Tan was lumbering further and further behind.

The tile-topped towers of the monastery came into view, then a wide archway with thrown-back wooden gates leading into a cobbled courtyard. Nick was waiting for her.

'Not in there.' Callie turned aside at the last moment, bypassing the gates and running into the monastery garden instead. It was alive with pink geraniums, orange bougainvillea and fragrant gardenia.

'The monks are gonna be convinced we don't want to see their monastery,' called Nick, running along beside her. 'Every time we get close we veer off in another direction.'

'We'll be cornered inside,' explained Callie breathlessly. 'Even with a coachload of tourists, Lobster Tan will think of something. And we can't turn ourselves in to the monks. They'd just hand us over to the police.'

The garden was contained within a thin, low wall which ran all the way round the monastery itself. On the other side of the flower garden was the monastery's fruit orchard with orange, peach and pomegranate trees. Callie ran straight into it and ducked down behind some large baskets of fruit.

'Do you think the monks would mind if we helped ourselves to some oranges?' asked Nick.

'Probably,' said Callie, 'but maybe if we leave them a donation...'

They collected enough fruit to fill Nick's backpack, and left three times as many euros than they would have paid at a shop. As Callie was putting the money in one of the baskets the familiar figure of Lobster Tan came panting into the orchard. He staggered a few more steps and then leant over with his hands on his knees, wheezing for breath. Callie ducked back behind the baskets just in time. 'Lobster Tan!' she mouthed to Nick. If he walked round the baskets he couldn't fail to see them.

'*Signomi...Signomi...*' Callie recognised the Greek word. It meant 'excuse me'. She put her eye to a thin gap between the baskets. She could make out a monk, wearing a dark belted cassock.

Lobster Tan's reply came from startlingly close to her. He had been just about to find them. '*Kalispera,* good afternoon,' he said.

'*Parakalo...* please.' The monk was beckoning. He wanted Lobster Tan to leave. '*Parakalo.*'

Lobster Tan started to follow the monk, but not before shooting a glance back at the baskets. Callie thought he knew exactly where they were hiding.

'We've got to find the back way out,' she whispered. Nick nodded.

Beyond the orchard wall there were areas of bare rock and dry yellow grass, and an impossibly steep slope. If they tried to run down it, they would never be able to stop! But with Skatelios and his men in the other direction, they didn't have a lot of choices.

'What do you reckon?' said Nick, peering at the slope.

'Suicide,' replied Callie.

'You go first then.'

Callie started shuffling down the slope on her backside, using her feet and the palms of her hands. It was slow but effective. 'Like this,' she called over her shoulder. Nick copied her and they managed to reach a line of trees after a few minutes. Callie scrambled to her feet. The ground was more level here.

A helicopter came storming low over the hillside with a high-pitched scream of its engine, and a rhythmical 'thwack thwack thwack' of its wide rotor blades. Crimson red, with a profile like a shark, it was cutting through the air at incredible speed.

The trees, and Callie with them, were hit by a shockwave of punched air. The helicopter jetted overhead with only metres to spare. It tipped on its side and circled the monastery.

Callie didn't need to read the words, but Nick read them anyway: 'Skatelios I'. It was emblazoned right down the side of the two-million-euro helicopter.

The helicopter rocked on its side again and angled off in the direction of the palace ruins.

Callie whispered, 'Come on.'

They followed the line of trees as far as they could downhill, almost another kilometre, until they reached open ground. The whitewashed houses of Villastoli were nestling in the bay below them. Yet between the trees and

Villastoli was another sloping area of scrub. If the helicopter returned, they'd be spotted right out in the open.

'Why don't we hide in that?' Nick was pointing at a vaguely conical rock formation.

'What?' How could they get inside a rock? Then Callie realised it wasn't a rock at all. It was a Greek windmill which had had its triangular canvas sails removed. It blended so naturally with the rock that it was virtually invisible. It was quite close to the trees, but still nearly a hundred metres to run. There would be a risk getting to it – the helicopter could be back any second.

'Do you think the helicopter's gone?' asked Nick, reading Callie's mind.

Callie listened hard for the sound of rotor blades. Even though she couldn't hear a thing, she answered, 'No.'

'Neither do I,' agreed Nick.

Callie made a decision. 'Look, just run as fast as you can, and don't stop until you get inside the windmill.'

Nick nodded.

'Now!'

They started running through low, thorny bushes which stung and scratched their legs.

'What if it's locked when we get there?' called Nick, when they were halfway there.

Callie plunged on. 'I don't suppose you could have mentioned that *before* we started running!'

The beat of the helicopter's rotor blades was back, throbbing through the air right behind them. *Skatelios I* was zeroing in on them. They were going to be caught.

Nick reached the windmill and disappeared from view. It wasn't locked, but Callie wasn't there yet! Five seconds later and she catapulted herself through the open doorway. She spun, expecting to see the helicopter looming large and on a collision course with the windmill. It was nowhere to be seen. She ran to a square window hole and scanned the horizon.

Skatelios I was only now lifting over the trees with a roar of its engines. It turned and curved away in the direction of the monastery again. It had failed to see the windmill and, better still, it had failed to see them.

Callie turned away from the window, leaned her back against the wall and slowly slid all the way to the floor.

'They could have left some bread or scones, or cake!' complained Nick in disappointment, ten minutes later.

Whoever owned the windmill had left very little at all. It was a shell, with even the millstone and the workings removed, maybe to be put to use somewhere else. All they'd left were a few empty flour sacks, full of holes. Callie arranged them into two mattresses for them to sleep on. They'd have to spend the night somewhere, and the windmill was a whole lot more tempting than a night under the trees. Tomorrow morning, before it got light, they could walk down to Villastoli. In the meantime they had oranges, peaches and pomegranates to eat, and the last bit of Callie's sausage roll.

'How long is it since we last heard the helicopter?'

asked Nick, peeling an orange.

'It must be at least twenty minutes,' estimated Callie. 'They could have landed and started searching on foot though.'

Nick shook his head. 'I reckon they've given up. For all they know, we sneaked out with the tourists. Lobster Tan knows how we operate.'

'Only too well,' replied Callie hollowly. It was her fault he'd caught them in the first place. If only she hadn't been looking at King Akanon's map in the hotel! They were going to have to be much more careful from now on. Skatelios obviously had people working for him all over the island – *anyone* could turn out to be an enemy.

'Skatelios knows where we're going to go next, though,' Nick went on.

Callie gave him a quizzical look. 'What makes you think that?'

'Lobster Tan looked at the maps.'

'He only glanced at them,' said Callie. 'He was too cocky to think we'd escape, so I don't think he really took them in.' She bit into a soft, blushing peach. 'What happened anyway, when I was down the well?'

'You must have been right at the bottom when he got there. I tried to fight him off but he was too big.'

Callie raised an eyebrow. Nick grinned immediately. 'I didn't hear him and before I knew what was going on he'd got his hand round my throat.'

'That's nothing. I fell right on my bum – at the bottom of the well,' grinned Callie.

'What was it like down there?'

'I don't think it was a well at all. It was just a place to hide the key, maybe in a part of the palace that only certain people were allowed to go...How did Lobster Tan know I was down there anyway?'

'You kept shouting, and he put his greasy fat hand over my mouth to stop me warning you.'

'Yuk.'

'Yuk's right,' said Nick, and stuffed more orange into his mouth. 'Show us the key then.'

Callie had completely forgotten it in the excitement. She drew it out of her backpack and handed it to Nick.

'I bet Skatelios went mental when Lobster Tan told him he'd given it back to us. He smacked his son in the face, just because he couldn't find us.' Nick turned the key, as if in an invisible lock. 'One down, two to go.'

'I hope the others are a bit easier,' said Callie.

'Yeah! Like that's gonna happen.'

Callie awoke with a heaviness across her chest. It was as if there was a weight pressing down on her. She opened her eyes and blinked in a glare of light. When she tried to look again she realised that a torch was pointed directly into her face. She dropped her gaze and saw a man's boot, planted firmly on her chest.

14
GREEK THEATRE
DRAMA

Glass Eye put more weight on his foot until Callie could hardly breathe. Lobster Tan Man was smacking Nick across the face to wake him up. 'Wakey wakey!'

Callie groaned. Lobster Tan hadn't given up after all. One of them should have kept watch!

'Tie wrap them,' ordered Lobster Tan. He fastened Nick's wrists together with a thin, clear plastic strip which looped through itself and then tightened into a ring that couldn't be pulled apart. Nick winced.

Glass Eye lifted his boot off Callie's chest and forced her wrists together. She tried to keep them slightly apart as he used one of the plastic tie wraps on her, and cried out before it really hurt.

'On your feet. Both of you,' Lobster Tan barked. He was angrier than before. He'd obviously lost a night's sleep searching for them.

As Callie struggled to her feet, she could feel the tie wrap biting into her wrist. It was tight but not tight enough! She would be able to work her hands free.

'Now get moving, and this time, *I'll* take the bag.'

Callie exchanged a helpless expression with Nick.

Lobster Tan sent Nick sprawling through the door of the windmill, landing on the ground outside.

'What was that for?' flared Nick, scrambling back to his feet.

'Because I felt like it!'

Glass Eye pushed Callie out after her brother. 'You want some too, Mees Latham?' The torchlight glinted off his artificial eye.

'No thanks.'

'I thought you didn't need us once you'd got the map,' Nick challenged Lobster Tan, as they stood outside the windmill in the dark.

Callie could have kicked him. What did he think Lobster Tan was going to do – just let them go?

'Oh, we've got some fun in store for you, Nicholas,' chortled Lobster Tan. 'Mr Skatelios is going to torture you to make your parents reveal exactly where King Akanon's Treasury is located.'

'Something for to look forward,' leered Glass Eye. Callie wondered if he meant for him or them.

'Let's go!' said Lobster Tan. He gestured which direction he wanted them to take with the beam of his torch. Tonight the moon had stayed resolutely hidden behind grey clouds. They started walking through prickly scrub, aiming for the distant lights of Villastoli, shimmering around the horseshoe bay far below.

'What if we walk straight off a cliff?' questioned Nick.

'Then you'll get down quicker, won't you?' Lobster Tan snapped back impatiently. 'Now get on with it.'

They were making slow progress. If there *was* a path

down from the windmill, they'd obviously missed it.

Callie was straining to see where she was going, while at the same time twisting her wrists back and forward to slowly work her hands out of the tie wrap. She bit her lip to stop herself gasping in pain, as the plastic cut into her skin. Suddenly she felt it slide off and fall unnoticed on the ground. She kept her wrists together and waited for a chance to escape.

They were getting closer to Villastoli village. The lights were clearer and the slope was levelling off towards the bay.

Lobster Tan suddenly let out a bellow and raked his torch at the scrub around his feet. Callie saw a snake as thick as her arm and almost two metres long slithering away from the light.

'I've been bitten!' cried Lobster Tan. 'A bloody big snake.'

He redirected the torchlight to his bare, sunburned leg. He was wearing shorts and the snake had struck him on the calf. 'Are they poisonous?'

'Mostly not,' said Glass Eye. 'Except—'

'EXCEPT WHAT?'

'Was it brown, with zigzagged marks?'

'It was!' lied Callie. The snake had been completely black. 'It slithered off that way.'

'OH GOD!' shouted Lobster Tan.

'Show me! Where did it bite you?' Glass Eye wanted to know.

Lobster Tan dropped the torch and Callie's backpack to show Glass Eye the bite on his calf.

Callie struck like a second snake, snatching up her discarded backpack and the torch. 'Run, Nick. Run!'

Callie darted off after Nick, fumbling with the torch switch. It went out and plunged them into darkness. She threw it as far away as she could and heard the lens smash against a rock. Lobster Tan wouldn't be able to follow them easily. Behind her, she heard him yell, 'LEAVE THEM! HELP ME!'

She grabbed Nick's arm and carried on running into the enveloping blackness.

'What are you eating?' Callie could hear Nick gnawing at something.

'This stupid tie wrap thing... How did you get yours off?'

'Just call me Callie Houdini.'

Callie was forcing the pace, tripping and stumbling over the uneven ground. They had no choice but to keep on for Villastoli. The next town along the coast would have been less obvious, but madness to attempt in the dark. There were obviously snakes on this part of the island!

The first hint of dawn was seeping into the sky as they started passing the whitewashed walls of houses on the edge of the town.

By the time Callie heard Nick's tie wrap finally snap, they were walking into the middle of Villastoli. 'Done it!' Nick whispered in triumph.

There were two hotels, one painted sky blue, the other

lemon yellow, and both had large shuttered doors opening onto balconies with black iron railings. A white church with an impressive bell tower was on an elevated spot, and several tavernas and a supermarket crowded the main street. Cars and mopeds were parked along either side. No one was about, apart from a stringy black cat dozing under a cherry tree.

Callie wondered how long they had before Lobster Tan and Glass Eye caught up with them. Somehow she didn't think Glass Eye's priority would be to get Lobster Tan to a hospital. Besides, when he didn't die from the snake bite, they'd realise it hadn't been a poisonous one.

Callie looked at a few of the lampposts. Their Wanted poster didn't seem to have made it to Villastoli.

'Skatelios could have asked people here to look out for us, though,' said Nick, guessing why she was suddenly peering at lampposts.

'I don't think he'd risk it,' said Callie. 'If we later turn up dead, he wouldn't want half the island coming forward and saying he was trying to catch us. The Greeks really like tourists, they're not going to think it's okay for Skatelios to start killing them just to get a treasure map.'

'And they probably think he's rich enough already,' added Nick.

Amazingly, somewhere was open. Villastoli Bakery had been working all night to make pastries and bread for their customers throughout the day.

'Looks like you're going to get bread and scones and cake after all,' said Callie.

160

At the bakery counter they seemed stunned to see anyone so early in the morning, let alone tourists, and bustled them proudly into the bakery itself. The massive ovens were blasting out a heat wave, and the smell of freshly baked bread made Callie's mouth water. 'What do you want?' she asked Nick.

Nick selected half the bakery's night's work for his breakfast. The round, smiling lady in charge, who seemed to be called 'Roula', even threw in an old knife and some goats' butter for free, so Nick could spread the bread instead of dipping it into olive oil the way the Greeks did.

She stroked his blond hair affectionately, and then pretended to spit.

'Eugh!' exclaimed Nick.

'She's warding off the evil eye,' whispered Callie. 'It's to protect you.'

'Yeah! But there's food about!'

'Shut up. We need all the protection we can get.' She beamed at Roula. Roula smiled back.

'Is there a taxi in Villastoli?' asked Callie, after they'd paid for all the bread and pastries. 'Taxi?' she repeated, when Roula and two men working the ovens looked blankly at her. She was sure the word 'taxi' was the same in Greek.

'SOFIA, SOFIA!' Roula started shouting.

A girl not much older than Callie, and with flour on her cheeks, came running in through a side door. Roula spoke to her in rapid Greek, and then Sofia smiled eagerly at them.

161

'Roula says I am to translate.'

'We want to hire a taxi?' explained Callie.

Sofia translated to the other three, who had all stopped working because this was much more interesting.

Roula's fond expression had changed, and she was now looking Callie and Nick up and down suspiciously. Callie realised they must look as if they were running away: buying food at the crack of dawn and asking where they could get a taxi.

'We've been lost in the hills all night,' she told Sofia, careful not to lie. 'Our parents will be worried about us, and we're trying to get back to them. All we need is a taxi.'

Sofia translated, and one of the men said something to the others, gesturing at a wall phone.

'We don't have the phone number where they're staying,' said Callie truthfully, 'and my dad broke his mobile phone last week so we can't ring him directly.'

Sofia translated again. After a pause, Roula shouted, 'THEO!'

Yet another member of the bakery staff appeared. He was burly and bear-like, with very little hair on his head but an amazing amount in his grey moustache. There was more gesticulating and pointing at Callie and Nick from everyone, and then Sofia asked, 'Which direction are you going?'

Callie had looked at the maps yesterday at the windmill. 'To Stenthos,' she said.

There was a little more discussion and then Sofia interpreted once more. 'Theo must make deliveries all the way to

162

Stenthos. He has agreed to take you, if you are ready now.'

Callie and Nick both nodded eagerly.

'Please, please. *Parakalo, parakalo,*' said Callie for both of them.

The road to the south-east corner of Thelta was one of the better routes on the island, freshly tarmacked, and nearly straight. It tracked the coastal strip, never threatening to climb into the mountains and their treacherous passes. It skipped past beach after beach with brightly coloured sun umbrellas and deckchairs, where no one was sunbathing this early in the morning. Only the occasional windsurfer was to be seen, zipping across the foam while hanging onto a bright sail.

The bakery van's cab was large enough for Callie and Nick to sit alongside Theo, who hadn't stopped chattering for the last half hour; speaking incomprehensibly for the most part, he'd suddenly inject a phrase like 'Buckingham Palace' or 'Manchester United' or 'Tesco's Supermarket'.

'I think he's been on holiday to England,' said Callie.

'Moussaka, The Acropolis, Olympiacos,' said Nick, naming a Greek dish he'd eaten last week, a famous landmark in Athens, and the only Greek football team he'd ever heard of.

Theo looked pleased. It seemed to be all the conversation he required. 'Prince Charles,' he replied.

'Kebabs,' said Nick.

They'd been travelling for ten minutes when they heard a car horn sounding impatiently behind them. Callie glanced into the bakery van's wing mirror and her heart almost stopped. They were being pursued by Glass Eye's brown saloon. Glass Eye himself was leaning on the horn. He wanted them to stop! How on earth could she tell Theo to put his foot down?

The road suddenly widened out and the saloon came hurtling past. Callie thought it was going to carve across their path and cut them off, but instead it sped on, clipping the kerb and raising a cloud of dust. Glass Eye and Lobster Tan were just in a mad hurry to get to Stenthos. They had no idea who was in the bakery van. Unfortunately, they were going to get to Stenthos ahead of them.

'Road hog!' commented Theo.

At Stenthos they left Theo delivering to a supermarket with thanks and handshakes, and then had him chasing after them to give them a final hug. Finally they hurried off as if eager to be reunited with their parents.

'We'd better not hang around anywhere too public,' said Callie, as soon as they were out of sight. 'Lobster Tan and Glass Eye could be anywhere.'

'Where's the next key?' asked Nick.

'If the calculations are right, it's somewhere it shouldn't be.'

'What does that mean?'

Callie sighed. 'It's at a Greek theatre – a Greek theatre which wasn't built until eight hundred years *after* King Akanon.'

'What!'

*

164

The theatre was set in the wooded foothills which surrounded the south-eastern corner of Thelta. Callie and Nick followed an uneven mud track from Stenthos, guided by brown and white signs written in Greek and English: *The Theatre of Stenthos*. It was still early but already there were tourists heading in the same direction.

'They're going to get there first,' groaned Nick.

'We probably won't get the place to ourselves until after dark,' reasoned Callie. 'But we can still look round for anything which might have been there *before* the theatre... In King Akanon's time.'

'Like a key chamber.'

Callie gave him a wry smile. 'If it's that obvious it'll already be empty... What we can do is work out what the clues on the clay tablet mean.'

She had copied the markings onto the back of the map print-out at the windmill, and was decidedly confused. There were two circles inside two squares, and a cross right between them. She thought the circles represented the sun and the moon, because one had little rays coming off it and the other had a crescent carved through the middle. But that was as far as she'd got.

They crested a rise and saw the theatre stretching up the hillside in front of them.

It was a massive theatre with a paved central area. At the edge a wall ran for almost two thirds of the way round to enclose the stage. The stage was big, but the auditorium was truly colossal. Stone seats ran thirty rows back, climbing high up the hill; each row a perfect semicircle, around the one in front of it. It was open to the elements, and had the rocks and sea below for scenery, and the sun above for lighting.

'Pretty uncomfortable,' Nick decided, plonking himself on the smooth, hard stone of one of the seats.

Callie sat on the row in front of him and started applying sun cream to her bare arms and face. 'What were you expecting? Sofas?'

'What are these notches for?' Every ten metres or so there was a notch, the size and shape of an open cat flap, between the seats. It was duplicated on each row, and every notch lined up with the one on the row behind it, all the way from the stage to the back of the auditorium.

'I don't know,' admitted Callie. 'Maybe it's to make it easier to find your seat. You know, row thirteen, notch ten...Come on, I want to see what that guide's saying down there.'

The tour guide was American, and in charge of a small group of adults who were also American. She had fearsome red hair which was short and permed into tight curls, and was wearing a uniform of a dark blue skirt and a floral blouse. She was drawling in a loud American accent.

'Although Stenthos Theatre was built in 423 BC, it displays some notable architectural peculiarities.'

Callie wandered to the edge of the group.

'What's she on about?' whispered Nick.

'Shhh.'

'Take the columns for instance—' the tour guide went

on. There were two high columns, lamppost high, one on either side of the centre circle. 'They're not typical of the classical period of Greece.'

'She's right,' whispered Callie, starting to feel excited. 'They're really plain, like the ones found in Mycenaean temples and palaces. Later on they often carved straight grooves all the way down their columns.'

'Speak up, dear. I'm sure we *all* want a piece of your expertise.'

Callie's face flushed red. The tour guide had said that just to embarrass her. She repeated her comment about the columns.

'Well, it seems you know a *little* about the subject,' conceded the guide.

'A little! She probably knows a lot more than you do!' flared Nick angrily.

Callie almost swung him off his feet as she pulled him away. 'Our mum and dad are over there,' she stammered, pointing vaguely to a crowd of complete strangers, and marching Nick towards them. 'Must go.'

'All right, all right, you can let go now,' said Nick, once they were out of earshot. 'I was only sticking up for you.'

'Never mind that. Those two columns are on the map. They *were* here during King Akanon's time, and I bet that means the centre circle was as well. Whatever it was used for originally, later Theltans must have adopted it as a theatre and added the seats. And when they did, they probably added the rows of notches from the lower level without ever understanding their purpose.'

Callie led the way to the outermost ring of seats at the top of the hill, where they couldn't be overheard. She sat down and fished around in her backpack for the map of Stenthos, and turned it over.

'Look, this is what's on the clay tablet.' She showed Nick what she'd copied down.

'I think it means trap the sun and moon in a box or something,' said Callie.

'*Or,* you line up the sun and moon with the notches, and the shadow from the columns makes a big cross and that's where you dig,' said Nick. This time it had taken him several minutes to work it out.

Callie's mouth fell open. They were sitting right next to one of the weird notches. From a certain angle it looked exactly like a box.

'You mean it's like a giant sundial?'

'What's a sundial?'

'Like you described – only the shadow points to what time it is.'

'Yep. That's exactly what I mean.'

Callie went quiet for a moment, thinking. Everything seemed to fit – all the clues, the location, even the oddly out of place columns. She glanced up at the sun. It was already high in the sky and was arcing higher. It wouldn't start descending towards the notches until the afternoon, and even then it probably wouldn't line up exactly until around sunset. Goodness knew what time the moon would line up. Finding this key wasn't going to be quick!

Callie noticed the guide and her small party of Americans climbing into a minibus in the dust patch of a car park. They must be heading off to another part of Thelta.

'Well,' she said with a smile, 'I think we're going to need something to dig with.'

'It's too heavy,' Callie told Nick, who wanted to buy a pickaxe. 'And it's hardly inconspicuous, is it, if we're spotted wandering around with pickaxes over our shoulders like two of Snow White's dwarves on their holiday in Greece!'

'But they don't have soil round here,' said Nick. 'They have *rock*.'

'We'll just have to manage,' said Callie finally.

They were arguing in a small hardware shop on the outskirts of Stenthos. The Greek customers were showing quite an interest in them. Callie hoped it was only because they didn't normally get tourists buying tools as souvenirs, and not because the police had circulated their poster.

'What about a spade then?'

'It's TOO big!'

They came out of the shop with two trowels, a ball of string and two tent pegs to mark out the shadows the sun and moon made. Callie looked right, and then stepped into the road to cross. Immediately she heard squealing tyres. In Greece they drove on the wrong side of the road. She saw the car coming straight at her, and it was a brown saloon.

15

SUN AND MOON

'Callie! Callie!'

Callie was lying on her back in the middle of the road. She slowly opened her eyes and saw a crowd of Greek faces staring down at her. Nick was on his knees shaking her. What had happened? Then she remembered. She was going to be run over by Glass Eye, but the brown saloon had barely touched her. She'd fallen over! It must have looked exactly like—

'I'm all right,' she told Nick. 'But we've got to get out of here.'

'How? I think they've called an ambulance.'

Callie saw Glass Eye pushing through the crowd. He bent down and gripped her under the arm to help her up. Lobster Tan was holding open the rear door of the car.

'We'll take you to the hospital,' he said. A couple of the Greeks started helping her into the car too. She had to do something before it was too late!

She shook Glass Eye off and rounded angrily on him. 'You maniac! You were driving too fast! You could have killed me!' She started gesticulating madly at him.

Nick joined in. 'Call the police! He's a dangerous driver!'

The Greek crowd began to get the message: the driver of the brown saloon had mown down the English girl.

They surrounded Glass Eye and Lobster Tan angrily, and started shouting at them. One of the crowd started kicking the car. Someone ran into the hardware shop to telephone the police. Traffic was backing up along the road.

Callie and Nick melted away unnoticed.

'How long do you think the locals will hold them for?' asked Nick, when they were safely out of the village.

'Not very long when they realise the casualty's gone.'

'Lobster Tan and Glass Eye won't be able hang around in Stenthos, though,' said Nick. 'Not after all that.'

'They also know we're here.'

They were walking back towards the theatre, past fields bordered by low rock walls and wire fences. A farmer was clearing rocks from one of the fields with a pickaxe. He smiled at them.

'You know what he's thinking?' said Nick.

'What?'

'He's thinking we should have got a pickaxe.'

'Oh, ha ha.'

There were still as many tourists at Stenthos Theatre when they got back, and they would have hours to wait yet before the sun lined up with the notches. Callie went to look at the columns again – properly this time. They weren't as plain as she'd first thought.

'Look!' Instead of the normal disc-shaped base, the entire column was supported on a carved lion's paw.

'Now we *know* we're in the right place,' said Nick.

They went to sit at the top level of seats again, nearest

the notch which would be first to line up with the sun. Then they waited...

It was late afternoon when Callie saw the police car bouncing up the rough track, leaving dust flying in its wake. It pulled into the small mud car park and stopped in the middle, as if was it too important to find a space between the rental cars and tour buses.

Horrifyingly, Khrisous was climbing out of one side, and the American tour guide out of the other. Callie understood instantly. 'She must have recognised us from the posters, and gone straight to the police.'

'But we didn't see any in Stenthos,' said Nick. 'Not one. Or at Villastoli last night.'

Callie shook her head. 'Maybe... Maybe she took her Americans to Thelta Town, and saw the posters there. It doesn't matter – she's led him straight to us! And if we run now, they're bound to spot us.'

'That's not the only problem,' said Nick. 'Look at the sun – any minute now and it's going to reach the first notch.'

Callie's throat felt suddenly dry.

Khrisous and the tour guide had walked over to the column closest to the car park. The tour guide was pointing out where Callie and Nick had been standing earlier, and then gesturing at the column. Khrisous gave it the merest glance, as if it could tell him nothing important, and then started to scan the rows of seats working from right to left. If he looked directly at where they were sitting...

172

'Excuse me... Would you take our photograph?' A middle-aged English couple had stepped right in front of Callie and Nick. It was as if a screen had been placed between them and Khrisous.

Callie found her voice. 'Yes, of course.' She stalled for time. 'You'll have to show me how the camera works first though.' She had to keep the couple precisely where they were!

'It's really simple,' said the middle-aged man. 'When you've got us on this little screen, just press here.' He showed Callie the shutter-release button.

Callie took the camera and examined it, as if making sure she understood exactly what to do. She slowly raised it in front of her face. 'Okay. Say "Greek Cheese"....'

The couple spoke together: 'Greek Cheese.'

'Oh hang on, I think you moved.' How much longer could she keep this up? As Callie used the camera once more, she could see Khrisous and the tour guide getting back into the police car. She handed back the camera as they drove away.

'Thank you,' said the middle-aged man.

'No. Thank *you*,' said Nick, beaming at him. *'Thank you, very much.'* The English couple walked away looking baffled.

Callie spun around to see where the sun was. Amazingly, they still had time, it was just slotting into the first notch on the back row of seating. Then it was immediately obvious that the sun wasn't going to line up with the column at all; it was at the wrong angle!

There was an agonising, fifteen-minute wait for the sun to reach the next sequence of notches, and again it failed to line up with either of the columns. The sun was dipping ever lower on the horizon. What if it went *under* the third notch, and didn't make a shadow at all, thought Callie frantically. It would be too low to make it to the fourth row of notches. This was their last chance.

'Why are we still up here?' asked Nick suddenly. 'Shouldn't we be near the column?'

'Oh God! You're right!' shrieked Callie. They raced down the seats as if they were steps, and ran to a column each. The minutes dragged on achingly.

Just as Callie had given up hope, it happened. She looked up and saw an unobstructed view through every single notch in the third row – it looked as though a tangerine globe was trapped inside a box. She turned away, half blinded by the glare.

Nick was already running down the length of the column's shadow as it stretched across the hardened ground beyond the theatre. Callie caught up with him and stared in astonishment at the shadow. The very tip looked like a lion's paw. The top part of the column must be carved to create the illusion. Then all at once the shadow vanished, and the sun dipped behind the back of the auditorium.

'Don't give you long, do they?' commented Nick.

Callie looked round. There were fewer tourists now, but still enough to observe what they were doing. She started to mark the spot with the toe of her trainer. Then she bent down as if tying her shoelace and started working the first tent peg into the soil. She stamped on it a couple of times as if checking her trainer was on firmly.

The sky was turning crimson, reflecting into the sea and making it look like red wine. No one was arriving any more. It was only people leaving, slowly, and in ones and twos. Now all they could do was sit down and wait for the moon to rise.

'What are you going to do with *your* treasure?' asked Nick, as they polished off the last of the bread and pastries from Villastoli bakery.

Callie was taken aback. 'What do you mean, *my* treasure. There's not going to be any *my* treasure,' she informed him primly. 'It's going to Andreas. At what point did you become confused?'

'How's he to know if we keep some of it?'

Callie shook her head in disbelief. 'That's what got Dad into this mess in the first place, Nick!'

'So you don't want a pony, or tickets to see Madonna, or your own car, then?'

Callie screwed up her face. 'No!'

'Oh.'

They had the theatre all to themselves now, and the moon had been rising steadily for the last hour. Any minute now…

The moon slotted into the first notch.

Callie groaned. It wasn't going to line up properly with the column. It wasn't even close. Mind-numbingly slowly, the moon continued to rise.

'How long is it now?' asked Nick.

'What? Since you last asked, or since the last notch?'

'The last notch.'

'Ages.' Callie leaned her back against the second column and stared up at the rows of empty seats. From here, she couldn't even see the moon! Or could she? 'Look!'

Iridescent light was shining around the edge of another notch. Callie held her breath. As she watched, the notch slowly filled with light.

There it was, a silver moon captured in a box. The column's shadow lengthened, like a lion's paw reaching out.

Callie and Nick raced to the very tip of the paw. Callie stamped the second tent peg into the ground quickly, and tied the string to it. The shadow disappeared seconds later.

'Well, now we're going to find out if you were right,' she said. She went back to the column and tied the other end of the string around it, so that it formed a straight line. Then she did the same with the remaining column.

'Find the first peg,' she shouted. 'I think it's that way, towards the trees.'

Callie started searching the ground, unwinding the string behind her. After a minute she realised she hadn't gone far enough. The two lengths of string had to cross! She could see Nick, bent low over the ground, miles away from where she was. One of them had to be looking in the wrong place. Maybe they both were. A sudden feeling of panic clutched at Callie's insides. What if this didn't work? What if there was no key at all?

'It's over here!' shouted Nick.

Callie looked up. He was in a completely different place from where he'd been a moment ago. She ran over to him, still unwinding the string. 'Where?'

'There look.'

Callie stooped down and saw that he was right. 'How on earth did you find it?'

'I left a bit of bread near it to help us. Look.'

There was a slice of crusted bread on the ground near the tent peg. Callie rolled her eyes. Blessed by the gods! 'If anyone else had done that some bird would have eaten it.'

She pulled the string as tight as she could and then tied it to the tent peg. They worked their way back to where the two strings intersected.

'Now the hard part,' said Nick. 'Digging through concrete with a dessert spoon . . . '

Callie opened her backpack and took out the two trowels she'd bought. She stabbed one at the ground. There was a metallic ringing sound, as if she'd struck the key at her first attempt. It was only the steel trowel on the concrete-hard ground.

'Told you!'

Callie tried again, a little further away. The trowel went in about a centimetre and she levered out a lump of hard soil. She looked at Nick. At this rate they'd still be here tomorrow morning when the tourists came back.

'Maybe it won't be very deep,' Nick said hopefully. He

tried using the other trowel and removed another small clump of soil.

After thirty minutes of hacking with the trowels, they'd made a hole the size of a dinner plate – but it was still only a few centimetres deep!

'I'm going to go and get a pickaxe,' said Nick firmly.

Callie almost laughed. 'The hardware shop's not going to be open now, it's nearly midnight.'

'I'm going to look in that field we went past, where the farmer was digging out rocks.'

Callie thought about it. It was a really good idea. 'Okay, but be careful.'

Nick sprinted away. She watched him until he disappeared over a ridge. A week ago she would have ppy to get rid of him for a while, but now all she could think was, 'I hope he's not very long.' It wasn't even because he might come back with a pickaxe; she'd started to rely on him – something she would never have believed possible a week ago.

Callie stared at her excavation trench. This wasn't the way archaeology was supposed to be – chipping away at baked soil under cover of darkness while on the run from a maniac and the Greek police. She started work again.

She carried on for another fifteen minutes, her hands becoming sore and blistered from the wooden handle of the trowel. Fifteen minutes. The field where the man had been clearing rocks couldn't be more than five minutes away. What was keeping Nick? Had he run into trouble?

Callie dropped the trowel and started running after Nick. She didn't get more than a few paces before she saw a figure, hunched and menacing, charging straight at her. Glass Eye! She froze on the spot. Where was Lobster Tan? Had he caught Nick?

'Don't just stand there. Give me a hand!' It was Nick's voice.

He lurched towards her, struggling with a pickaxe over one shoulder and a spade over the other. 'What's up with you? You look like you've seen a ghost.'

Callie managed to find her voice again. 'You've got it! Now we really do stand a chance.'

'He'd left his shed unlocked, but I couldn't find what I was looking for at first. Then I decided to bring the spade as well. I left some money so he could buy new ones, and a lock for his shed,' Nick told her.

They went back to the hole they'd already made, and Nick took charge of the pickaxe. Working together, it didn't take long to enlarge the dig. Nick was breaking up the ground with the pickaxe, while Callie dug the soil out with the spade.

The metal point of the pickaxe suddenly rang out on something that sounded like rock or stone.

'Hang on a minute.' Callie went back to using the trowel, scraping away the loose soil. She heard something stone-like grating under the trowel's blade.

Nick dropped the pickaxe and started using the other trowel. At first it looked like the stone was just an obstruction, no different from those the farmer had been lifting from his field. Then they began to reveal carved edges.

'It's a paw!' said Nick loudly. 'A lion's paw!'

Callie trembled. Once more she could feel the presence of King Akanon.

'But there's no key,' Nick added, digging desperately around the sides of the paw.

'I bet the lion's holding the key in its paw!' said Callie. 'We've got to turn it over.'

They worked one point of the pickaxe underneath the edge of the lion's paw, and then pulled the pickaxe handle like a lever. The stone flipped over with a thud. Underneath was a key-shaped socket, and shining dully in the middle of it was the second bronze key. It was exactly the same size as the first, but the arrangement of teeth was completely different. Nick picked it up.

'What's the matter?'

Callie had sprung round. She could hear a car on the track leading up from the village. As it appeared over the horizon, its headlights sprayed the hillside like search-lights.

'Get down!' Callie threw herself flat on the ground. She was relieved to see Nick do the same.

There were three cars climbing up the track, a green jeep, a brown saloon and lastly, a gold-coloured Mercedes Benz – all three she had seen before. It was Skatelios and his private army. They were driving into the small car park at the side of the theatre, and if they turned to park along the front edge, their headlights would be pointing straight at them. They would be seen even though they were lying flat on the ground.

'Hang onto that key!' Callie whispered urgently. 'We've got to get to the trees before they turn.'

She only half got to her feet and aimed for the trees in a low scrabbling run. Out of the corner of her eye she could see the headlights starting to sweep across the ground towards them as the three cars turned. With only seconds to spare, she flung herself under cover. Nick was right beside her.

The cars stopped and left their lights blazing as everyone got out: Andreas, Lobster Tan and Georgiou Skatelios. Glass Eye was bringing up the rear, forcing Callie's parents in front of him with the barrel of a machine gun. Callie could see her dad was trying to keep himself between the machine gun and her mum.

'It's Mum and Dad!' cried Nick. *'They're all right.'*

'He needs them. How else could he have worked out where to come?'

'Khrisous could have tipped him off,' said Nick.

Callie nodded. 'Maybe he's just hoping they'll show him where to dig.'

Skatelios had marched over to the columns. He seemed to spot the string immediately, stooping down to slip his hand underneath it and then following it a short way. He pointed to the other column and yelled something at Andreas.

Andreas ran over to the second column and quickly found the string. Skatelios had continued to follow the first string along, and stopped at the hole only seconds before Andreas. It took Skatelios only an instant to realise he was too late. Glass Eye caught up with them and stared into the empty hole. Skatelios yanked the machine gun away from him, and fired a long, insane burst into the hole. The sound of bullets clattered wildly around the hills.

'He's mental!' said Nick. 'A complete asylum case.'

Skatelios lifted the barrel of the machine gun and blasted away into the trees. Callie and Nick threw themselves flat again as bullets raked the branches above them. Callie was covering her head with her hands and screaming as leaves and splinters of bark showered her.

It was only a sickening moment of Skatelios-rage, because the firing stopped just as abruptly as it had started.

When she was brave enough, Callie lifted her head from the ground and peered out through the trees. Skatelios and Andreas were heading back to the cars. Glass Eye and Lobster Tan were pushing Callie's parents between them.

At the last moment before reaching the gold Mercedes, Skatelios stopped and glowered at the trees.

'He can see us!' whispered Nick.

Callie's flesh crawled. It was as if she was staring right into Skatelios's eyeballs.

He still wasn't climbing into his car. Instead he motioned to Glass Eye. Glass Eye side-footed Callie's dad behind the knee, making him kneel in front of him. Her dad twisted cat-like, ready to spring up and defend himself, then stopped as Skatelios rapped the side of his head with the point of the machine gun.

Skatelios's American-accented voice suddenly echoed around the theatre. 'Little girl...! Don't make me kill your father... Your interference places both him and your mother in jeopardy. Surrender to me before I am forced to harm them.'

Callie realised just in time that Nick was about to run out of the trees. She wrestled him back before Skatelios could see him. 'Nick! No! It's what he wants you to do.'

'He's going to kill Dad!' Nick shouted at her.

'Not until he gets the keys and the map! He still needs Mum and Dad to work out where the last key is. If we give ourselves up, he can kill us all!'

Nick looked tortured by indecision.

'You have to trust me, Nick.'

Finally, Nick nodded. He'd trusted her so far.

'Look,' said Callie. Skatelios had thrown the machine gun back to Glass Eye, and was climbing into the gold Mercedes.

Callie felt the tears staining her cheeks. It had all been a bluff.

16
FOLLOW THE RIVER

In her dream, Callie was standing in The Temple of the Leonotaur on ancient Thelta.

Princess Electra, sister of King Akanon, was dressed in bright blue skirts and a yellow bodice. Her dark hair was tied back with strings of pearls and delicate gold wire. She was, unusually, quite alone, without guard or serving maid.

She was walking slowly down a long, shallow staircase, between two columns of ruby red pillars. The Leonotaur's temple was buried so deep beneath the earth that no natural light could penetrate so bronze oil horns adorned the walls, the oil aflame and producing a flickering light.

Silently, tears began to flow down Electra's soft, pale cheeks.

Callie realised that news had reached Thelta that King Akanon's ship, The Lion, had been lost in a storm, and with it, the Princess's beloved brother. Electra had won the honour of sacrificing herself to the Leonotaur, the lion-headed monster, so that the gods might grant her one last life wish – to deliver her brother safely from the sea. If it was not too late.

Electra's sandalled feet reached the final step and carried her through the gateway to the Leonotaur's palace. Inside, the passageway narrowed, but the walls were painted the same vivid red colour, like a coat of blood.

Callie followed as Electra took a timid step forward, and then another, and another. They were walking haltingly through a maze of tunnels. Sometimes they happened across a small chamber or room. One was furnished with a couch and the floor was strewn with silk cushions of vibrant colours; while another was completely circular with a sapphire blue pool and had dolphins ridden by sea fairies painted on the wall.

At last, Electra's hesitant steps led them to a room with a disc-shaped stone table inlaid with marble at its centre. It was the lion-headed monster's sacrifice chamber, and the table was his altar. Opposite the entrance was a great golden door resting on golden wheels fitted into a track along the floor.

After a deep breath, Princess Electra climbed onto the altar disc and settled herself in a kneeling position. She arranged her skirts about her and began to intone her prayer:

'O hear me, O Gods,
Proud Thelta weeps for its mighty Lord, King Akanon –
My brother and my protector.
Accept the life from my body,
That King Akanon may return once more.'

There was a great rumbling sound, and the golden door began to roll aside. Princess Electra remained kneeling in awe and terror, trembling uncontrollably. Callie trembled *with her. None but the monster could open that door.*

Callie felt helpless and AFRAID.

The gate was fully open now and the monster towered above Princess Electra, above Callie – the heavily muscled body of a man and the amber-eyed head of a lion. The Leonotaur gave a bellowing roar and sprang forward.

Princess Electra buried her face in her skirts...

Callie awoke in a cold sweat, and for a moment had no idea where she was. Then she saw the sunlight flooding in through the square hole which passed for a window. Last night, after Skatelios's hail of bullets, they had walked for an hour and found a small stone shelter with a rusted corrugated iron roof. They had spent the rest of the night sleeping on broken hay bales.

Rubbing the sleep from her eyes, Callie went to the window. The sun was already high. They must have slept late.

She left Nick sleeping and went outside, taking her backpack with her.

In the sunlight she saw that the stone shelter was on a shallow slope, overlooking the south coast of the island. Long, dry grass waved like a cornfield.

Callie sat on a wooden bench along the front of the shelter and opened her backpack. There was a clink as the two bronze keys knocked together. She removed them and examined them minutely. They had the same lion-head moulding on one end but a different pattern of teeth on the other. Callie thought they were quite beautiful, and at the same time a terrible burden. Men would kill for these keys, and a kingdom had fallen for the want of them; and still, there was a third hidden somewhere out there to the west.

She pulled up some handfuls of dried grass from around the shelter and used it to wrap the keys before returning them to her backpack. Then she opened the last of the maps she'd printed. The place marked simply as '*Nekrotafio*' was nearly thirteen kilometres from Stenthos. They must have covered five last night. If they hadn't been so tired they might have pushed on all the way, before Skatelios could get ahead of them, because now, for the first time, he would be certain of which direction they were headed.

Even Nick had worked it out. 'Now there's only one key left we're bound to head west. Skatelios could be waiting for us anywhere along the way,' he'd pointed out last night.

They couldn't trust their lives to seemingly friendly locals either. Anyone might report them to the police – even American tour guides!

'I've got breakfast up,' said Nick, stumbling out of the shelter. 'I bought some Greek chocolate bars, Coca-Cola and crisps from the supermarket in Stenthos yesterday.'

'I knew I shouldn't have let you do the shopping,' said Callie. Even so, she ate some crisps and a little piece of chocolate. She leant her back against the rough stone wall of the shelter, and closed her eyes to let the sun gently warm her face.

She jerked her head up again. What was that? Her entire body was shaking, and she could feel a strange rumbling under her feet. It was as if a heavy lorry had thundered past, shaking the earth.

Callie leapt to her feet, expecting to see something like an earth mover or a ten-ton truck bearing down on the shelter to flatten it, though when she looked round there was nothing at all. The hillside with its softly waving grass looked as peaceful as it had a moment ago, and the ground was no longer shuddering.

'Was that what I think it was?' cried Nick, glowing with excitement.

'If you mean an earthquake, I don't think it was a proper one. It was more of an earth *tremor*.'

'It still counts though!' enthused Nick. 'They'll be so jealous at school.'

Callie stared at him in astonishment. 'Last night we were nearly cut in half by machine gun bullets, and your *What I Did in My Holidays* essay is going to be about a two second earth tremor which probably nobody else on the island even noticed.'

'Who said anything about an essay? I'm going to the Sunday papers with my story.'

Callie raised an eyebrow. 'Let's just get off the island with Mum and Dad first, shall we?'

They were underway again. Apart from some wild goats and a mountain eagle soaring high above them, they'd seen no living creature in an hour's walking.

Callie smelt it first – the faint tang of burning on the wind. Maybe there was a Greek farm somewhere, burning stubble like they did in England, to get rid of the corn stalks after harvest. She tried not to think about it. It was probably nothing.

'Why's it doing that?' Nick was squinting at the horizon. It was quivering and blurring, a heat haze in every direction.

'I don't know,' said Callie, 'but we should keep moving.'

'I think you're right. Look!' Nick was pointing towards a dim, red glow. 'The field's on fire!'

Flames were sweeping in towards them from behind and both sides, shrivelling up the grass and creating a wall of smoke.

'This way!' Callie yelled, and started to run in the only direction remaining.

She could guess what was happening. Skatelios had torched the grass, and he was forcing them to go where *he* wanted. Was he playing with them? He might be disappointed yet. The gap they were running for was getting smaller and smaller. Callie could already feel the heat on her skin and hear the grass crackling behind her. Soon it would be her! 'Faster, Nick! Faster!'

She didn't care if she ran straight into Skatelios's arms. It had to be better than burning alive. She charged on through the long grass.

Miraculously they were out-running the flames. She could see a shallow river, acting like a firebreak a hundred metres ahead. They had to reach it. She thought about dropping her backpack to let the flames destroy the keys and the clay tablets for ever, but probably neither would burn, and Skatelios would still have them.

Run! Run! She was screaming to herself. Then somehow she had reached the river and was splashing straight into it and out on the opposite bank. Nick was close behind her.

She fell to her knees in exhaustion, but somebody was pulling her back up immediately.

'GET UP! GET UP!' And then unbelievably, 'Run that way! Follow the river.'

It was Andreas. He was half dragging her, half pushing her.

'My father has lost his mind. He wants me to trap you here while he brings up his hunting dogs.'

Callie remembered Manolis had told them that Skatelios hunted rabbits on the southern plains. They were going to be the rabbits.

'If you stay with the water, the river will take you west.' Andreas was still trying to force her back into the river. Callie looked into his haunted eyes. His father would make him pay big time for letting them slip past.

'Thank you,' she croaked.

'Go! Go!' Andreas implored.

'Come on, Callie,' Nick begged. 'COME ON!'

Callie started to run again, losing sight of Andreas in acrid black smoke.

The water was no more than ankle deep but uneven and slippery from the rocks that had rolled into it from the hills along one bank.

'We'll never outrun dogs,' Callie shouted.

'Well, *I'm* gonna try!' Nick called back.

Callie shot a glance over her shoulder. The field was still ablaze and there was no sign of dogs on the hill. 'How many dogs do you think he's got?'

'Including Glass Eye? Probably lots.'

It wasn't long before they heard the sound of baying dogs. Then, unexpectedly, the sound receded.

'They're going the wrong way!' panted Nick.

'Andreas! He's bought us some time.'

'Then let's use it!' exploded Nick.

They continued following the river which was now flowing between hills on either side.

It was five more minutes before they heard the dogs again.

'Skatelios must have worked it out!' moaned Nick. 'I bet he's pretty mad with Andreas.'

Callie glanced over her shoulder expecting to see the dogs. 'I don't know how much further I can go,' she groaned. Her muscles were screaming in pain, and the bronze keys and clay tablets in her backpack made it feel as if she was carrying a sack full of rocks.

'Give *me* the bag,' said Nick. 'I'm not as tired as you are.'

Callie thought he was lying to help her, but she wriggled gratefully out of the pink backpack, and handed it over. They kept on running.

In the time it had taken to swap over the backpack, the

sound of barking dogs had got louder. A moment later they saw them! Six in all: three rottweilers, an Alsatian and two of an enormous breed Callie didn't recognise. They threw themselves as a pack around a gap in the hills. Skatelios was right behind on horseback. On a second horse was Glass Eye, hanging on with difficulty. There was no sign of Andreas. Whatever Skatelios had done to him, he had been unable to continue.

The water was becoming deeper, above Callie's knees. She was soaked to the waist from running, but the banks on either side were steep. They would never get away from the dogs and horses that way. They must stay with the river.

'*There is no escape.*' It was Skatelios's American-accented voice, shouting after them. Callie could hear horses' hooves splashing in the water. The pack of dogs were clamouring for the kill. Skatelios would never order them off. All he wanted was the clay tablets and the keys – the dogs could have the rest.

'Argh!' Nick had plunged underwater right where he'd been running. His head bobbed back up a second later. The river had got deeper, and Nick was being carried away by the current. They might get away yet. But only if they started to swim!!!!

Skatelios suddenly woke up to the same possibility. He was whipping his horse viciously, kicking its flanks with his booted heels, his face twisted in rage and hatred. He left Glass Eye far behind him.

'STOP STOPPPPPP!' He barked as viciously as any of his dogs. His horse's hooves were about to land on top of Callie, and the dogs were swimming after her. She had no choice. She had to swim!

She waded forward until the current took her too. The one Alsatian strained to keep its black and brown head above water and swam after her, while the other dogs frantically tried to reach the riverbank. Callie was barely swimming. The river was doing all the work.

She realised with a shock that she couldn't see Nick anymore. He had gone under again. The backpack! The weight of the bronze keys and clay tablets must have dragged him down! She struggled to swim against the current to where she'd last seen him, and found him grasping for the surface. She was only going to get one chance at this, before she was swept past... It was a lucky grab. Her fingers wrapped around the strap of the backpack and her momentum pulled it loose, and Nick's head clear of the water.

They were carried on together, dragging the backpack between them – neither daring to let it go. The Alsatian stayed with them, paddling beside Callie – no longer chasing, just trying to save itself.

The river surged through a gorge. Vertical rock walls accelerated the water, hurling them around submerged rocks. The water swirled Callie out of control and she thought she was going to be pulverised against a jagged rock, but the current changed direction at the last minute and she shot past. Finally the water poured into a wider section of river and a shelf of grey rock opened out at the edge.

'Make for the ledge.' Callie swallowed a mouthful of water nodding towards the bank. They swam as hard as they could and managed to drag themselves and the backpack out of the water.

The Alsatian started to panic in an effort to follow them, knowing it would be carried on by the river. Nick waded back in and grabbed it by the scruff of the neck before pulling it to safety. The dog's thick black and brown coat was slicked down from the point of its muzzle to the tip of its tail. It looked up at Nick sheepishly and nervously wagged its tail.

'What did you do that for?' Callie asked.

'I'm going to keep him.'

'Dad'll go nuts!' Callie started, and then pulled herself up. She sounded ridiculous. Dad would probably let them keep all of Skatelios's dogs, and his horse as well, if they could open the Treasury and pay off Andreas.

'I'm going to call him Skatelios.'

'Skatelios?' spluttered Callie.

'Don't you think it looks like him?'

'NO!'

'Well, I'm still calling him that.' Nick fed 'Skatelios' a soggy bar of chocolate from his pocket. Skatelios wolfed it down greedily.

'He reminds me more of you,' grinned Callie.

'Do you want any?' Nick offered the chocolate to Callie.

'No. Yuk!'

'You're probably right,' Nick agreed, with his mouth

full of the other half of Skatelios's bar. 'It's awful.'

Callie was looking in her backpack. The keys and the clay tablets were safe, though the printed maps had turned into papier-mâché, as all the coloured ink had run together to make one new colour, mushy brown. The map from the shop had fared slightly better. The river was marked, and so was Nekrotafio. They were literally just a spear's throw from the third key.

17

THE KING'S TOMB

There was nothing at all at Nekrotafio. It was just a plain hillside with coarse grass, pink rock roses and not one Mycenaean feature in sight.

'Maybe I got the coordinates wrong.' Callie's voice sounded distant.

Nick shook his head loyally. 'You couldn't have, or all the other coordinates would have been wrong.'

Callie was taken by surprise. Was her annoying little brother actually praising her? She sat down on the grass and took out the final clay tablet. Nick looked over her shoulder. The symbol for Nekrotafio resembled a circular maze with the figure of a lion in the centre. 'Maze,' he declared.

'So where is it?'

'Down there.' Nick pointed at the ground.

Callie shook her head. 'We can't dig up an entire hillside.'

'Maybe we'll find a way in, like an entrance or something,' said Nick.

Callie doubted it. It couldn't be that easy. Half an hour of searching confirmed it. They hadn't turned up anything remotely like an entrance. She sat down on the grass again. What they needed was her parents' geophysical equipment, so that they could see exactly what was

beneath their feet, like a giant x-ray. Callie attempt
think, but a few metres away, Skatelios was barking.

'What is it, boy?' called Nick. 'What's the matter?'

For a moment Callie thought Skatelios was asking for
more chocolate, then she realised he was barking at the
ground. 'He's as mad as his owner,' she concluded. She
went over to look. There was just short, dry grass, not
even a beetle to offend the dog. Then she felt it too. The
ground was shuddering.

'I think it's another—'

Callie had been about to say 'earth tremor' when something like an explosion went off under her feet.

The hard, dry ground tore upwards in front of her,
cracking open like an eggshell. She was cast violently to
the quaking ground. She could see Nick on all fours trying
to get to her. The noise was deafening, and the hillside was
ripping itself apart, piece by piece. Loose rocks hurtled
down the hill and smashed into the sea below.

The ground seemed to lift Callie and then drop her
back down. It stammered and rolled. She attempted to
cry out but her voice was drowned by the roaring of the
earth. Her teeth were rattling inside her head and her
vision was blurred by the extreme jolting of her body.

'Make it stop! Make it stop!' she screamed, no longer
certain whether she was saying the words out loud.

Then it did. The earth was suddenly still again, and all
that was left of the terrible noise was the ringing in her
ears.

A giant crack had ripped across the hillside, and lumps

of earth along the edges were still crumbling into it. Callie came to her knees unsteadily. 'Nick?'

'I'm here,' Nick said groggily. He looked as if he had just thrown up.

'Still like earthquakes?' she asked hoarsely.

Nick gave her a wry smile. 'Not much.'

They remained on their knees for some moments, amazed to be alive. Then Nick started to call, 'Skatelios. Skatelios...'

Callie looked around. Skatelios was gone. The last she'd seen of him he'd been standing right where the ground had opened up.

'Careful, Nick!' she yelled, as he dashed forward with the same thought. He stretched out onto his stomach and peered into the gaping rift.

'Skatelios...' he called again. 'Skatelios...' And then, 'I can't see him.'

With disbelief, Callie found she still had Manolis's torch and switched it on. Hoping the broken earth in front of her wasn't about to collapse, she knelt down and aimed the beam. What she saw stole her breath away. There was an ancient chamber right beneath them. It was decorated with fighting warriors on one side, and stacks of skeletons on the other. The earthquake, or perhaps even the gods, had revealed a Mycenaean tomb.

'Nekrotafio,' she breathed. 'Look.'

Nick crawled over to where Callie was, and peered down. 'Oh – WOW!'

'Stay here,' Callie said. 'I'll go and see what I can find.'

'I'd better go with you. He might not come to you.'

For a moment she didn't understand what he was talking about, and then she realised he meant the dog. 'Okay...But let me go first. I'll try and find the best way down.'

She slid her legs into the crack and then started to climb. The jagged edges of earth gave her places to put her hands and her feet, and then there was an easy drop down onto a layer of soil and rubble.

'It's really easy,' she called up, forgetting Nick was no climber. He finished his descent by falling on top of her.

'Nick!'

'Have you found him yet?'

'No!' Callie hadn't even looked round. 'He can't be hurt or he would have stayed put.'

There was a lot more light in the chamber itself. The opening was acting like a long, narrow skylight. Callie forced herself to look at the skeletons stacked from the ceiling to the floor on shelves carved right into the natural rock.

'Bodies!' said Nick with relish. 'It's like a CD rack of the dead.'

Each skeleton was armed with a round shield, a short, flat sword and a long, bronze spear. 'They're Mycenaean warriors,' said Callie. It was confirmed by the battle scene painted on the wall.

She hesitated. There was a doorway at either end of the chamber. 'Which way?'

Nick pointed. 'That way.'

Nick's doorway led into a long, thin tunnel which curved away in front of them. The roof was intact and they needed Manolis's torch to see their way. The walls were decorated with pictures, contained inside colourful borders like frames. There were pictures of a dark-haired woman carrying a water pitcher, a man riding on a turtle's back, two men wrestling, another throwing a javelin, and finally a man leaping over a charging bull. 'It's like an art gallery,' breathed Callie.

Another archway led them into a chamber like the first, where more skeletons were slotted into tombs cut into the wall. A painting depicted women wearing fine robes, and reclining by a pool in a formal garden. The women's faces were painted in white, whereas all the men's faces had been painted in dull red. The skeletons bore the crumbling remains of jewellery around their necks, and wrists, and ankles.

'So what are these?' asked Nick. 'The warriors' girlfriends.'

'They probably are,' replied Callie. 'Or their wives.'

They followed another long curving tunnel with more scenes from life in Mycenaean Thelta: charioteering, palace-building, a painted golden gateway, and a lion-hunt. It led on into a third chamber, where the painted wall showed older, bearded and finely-robed figures in lively debate, and the skeletons wore chains of office around their necks.

'Mycenaean counsellors,' concluded Callie.

'This one's the mayor,' said Nick, poking the skeleton with the most ornate chain.

'Counsellors, not councillors!'

'What's the difference?'

'Counsellors give advice. Councillors tell you what to do.'

'I bet you anything there's another curving tunnel at the end,' said Nick.

This time there were pictures of a golden ship being rowed across the ocean, a beautiful woman playing a stringed instrument, and a grapevine heavy with bunches of grapes. They wandered through and into the next chamber.

'It's like the first one,' said Callie, 'sliced through by the earthquake.' There were more warriors and the same picture. 'Wait a minute. It *is* the first one!'

'Skatelios couldn't have fallen in then,' said Nick, suddenly remembering the dog.

'And we didn't find the key either,' said Callie. 'We must have missed a turning,' she added, even though she was sure they hadn't. She looked around the chamber again. Nothing. No doors leading off apart from the two they'd already been through. She went back into the first picture gallery, playing the torchlight onto the tiled floor and walls in the hope of finding a secret door. Nothing. She carried on to Nick's chamber of warriors' girlfriends. One door in, one door out. The picture gallery after was as before – a single curving tunnel. They walked through the counsellors' chamber and were almost back to the beginning again.

'We're just going round in circles!' Nick told her.

'I know!'

'Maybe we should look at the map again?'

Callie fished around in her backpack and produced the clay tablet. The maze showed a series of concentric circles connected by small passageways at right angles.

'There's supposed to be a second ring inside the first,' she said. Then she suddenly realised: 'The painting! We've walked past the door twice.'

'What? Have we?'

She pelted back to the second curving gallery and stopped in front of the painting of the golden door. It didn't *look* any different from any of the other paintings. She examined it with the torch beam and ran her hand over the surface. It was perfectly smooth and cold to the touch. There were no hidden door handles or door knobs. She tapped her knuckle along a section of the wall. Right where the door was painted, it sounded hollow.

'We need something to break through with.'

'We could use this,' said Nick, and waved a sword at her.

Callie stepped back. 'Where did you get that?'

'I borrowed it from one of the skeletons. I had to prise it out of his—'

'Never mind!' Callie stopped him. 'Just use it.'

Nick raised the sword two-handed above his head, and swung it at the painting of the door. It smashed straight through, and revealed the opening to a passageway. Callie almost let out a cheer.

'So that's how you play,' said Nick.

Callie stepped inside and walked a few steps to another

junction. She shone the torch through and saw a second ring, running right inside the first. There were more brightly coloured images on the curving wall: warriors, eagles, warships and almost immediately, a painting of an archway with two lions guarding it.

Nick wielded the sword without waiting. There was a heavy clank, and all that happened was a tiny lump of coloured plaster was chipped out.

Callie tapped the painting of the archway with her knuckle. This time there was no hollow sound. 'It's solid.'

'No! Really?' said Nick, massaging his arm.

They walked on. After images of Zeus, and a three-headed dog, they came to the painting of an ordinary-looking wooden door. Callie tapped it. It made a decidedly hollow sound. 'Okay.'

As Nick raised the sword, the painting seemed to rush at him. He staggered back against the wall, and Callie was thrown onto her hands and knees. She felt the floor vibrating, and there was a deafening CRACK above her head. Another earthquake was going to bury them alive.

'SMASH IT, NICK! SMASH THE PAINTING!'

Nick swung the sword, and the painting shattered. Callie lurched to her feet and rammed him into the tunnel in front of her. Behind her tons of rubble exploded into the curving gallery like a bomb blast. The whole tomb continued to shake for almost a minute after. When the roofing blocks finally stopped crashing down, Callie could see there was no way back. How were they going to get out again?

Callie wiped the dust off the torch lens and headed in

the only direction left to them – into the third ring.

It was slightly different. The pictures were scenes from a Mycenaean king's life, from birth to death: a baby being held aloft by a man and woman wearing gold crowns; a boy practising with sword and shield; a youthful man driving a war chariot, long black hair flowing out behind him; the same figure having a crown placed on his head amidst many courtiers; then a king being carried on a bier of shields, a spear piercing his heart. The final scene was of a funeral. A sarcophagus, a stone coffin with a lion sculpture on the lid, was surrounded by weeping women and warriors, and two children: a golden-haired boy and a girl with dark-coloured hair. Callie knew who they must be – King Akanon and Princess Electra. The man whose life was depicted on the walls was their father – the former king of Thelta.

No wonder King Akanon had placed one of the keys here. Who better to protect it than his own father?

Right beside the sarcophagus scene was the painting of a dark tunnel. Callie tapped it. It was hollow. She nodded at Nick, and he smashed it to smithereens with the sword. Callie took a step forward, and found herself being heaved back. 'Wait!'

'What is it?'

Nick pointed with the sword.

Callie aimed the torch into the passageway.

'I can't see anything.'

'Exactly!' exclaimed Nick. 'Where did the pieces from the wall go?'

Callie looked again. The passageway didn't have a floor. It was a sheer drop – a trap! 'Thanks,' she said, swallowing a sudden lump in her throat.

There were no more images of doors. Everything else depicted scenes from King Akanon and Princess Electra's father's life.

'I've got an idea.' Callie began tapping the wall every few centimetres. It returned the same solid knock every time until—

'That was it!' Nick said unnecessarily.

Callie was staring at the wall in dismay. The passageway was right behind the painting of King Akanon and Princess Electra. They were going to have to destroy it to claim the final key.

Nick started to raise the sword.

'Wait!' Callie commanded. She opened her backpack and pulled out the black plastic bag Khrisous had given them their things in. It was folded into a very small, very neat packet.

'What's that?' asked Nick.

Callie unfolded it and reached right down to the bottom to take out her mobile phone. After all that time in the river, it was perfectly dry and unharmed. Callie switched it on, willing there to be some battery left. One tiny bar remained. She selected the camera, and started taking pictures of King Akanon and Princess Electra, until finally, the phone gave out. She looked at the painting one last time and hoped King Akanon would understand that what they were about to do was to save her parents.

'Go on then,' she sighed. King Akanon and Princess Electra disappeared in the stroke of Nick's blade.

Callie rewrapped her mobile carefully in the plastic bag and slipped through the newly opened archway. It led into a vault, circular and maybe ten metres across. Around the sides were alcoves, each housing a statue of a lion leaping in attack, teeth bared, claws extended and raking the air. Callie started as the movement of the torchlight made one of the lions appear to pounce at her. In the centre of the vault was the sarcophagus with an entire stone lion resting right on top of the lid.

'How are you supposed to open it with that thing on top?' asked Nick practically. 'It must weigh a ton.' He tried to prise the lid off with the blade of his sword. It barely lifted. He let it drop back down with a stony crunch.

Callie sat down on the floor with her back to the sarcophagus, feeling defeated. If they retrieved the key, how were they going to get out of here anyway? They were trapped, entombed.

Nick sat down between two of the pouncing lions and started practising his swordplay, with several lethal swishes of the blade. Clonk. He'd taken a lump out of one of the stone lions. Nick put the sword down guiltily.

Callie rested the back of her head against the sarcophagus, and aimed the torch at the vault ceiling. It had been constructed by placing overlapping block on top of overlapping block, to form a giant dome. There was a deep crack running right across the middle. Callie followed it with the beam from the torch. If the roof caved in, they could get out. And – the stone blocks would smash right through the sarcophagus lid. Callie wondered . . . ? It didn't look as if it would take much. She made up her mind.

'We're going to bring the roof down.'

'We're going to *what*?'

Callie shone the torch on the wall opposite the entrance. Swords and spears were piled up for the dead King to use in the afterlife. 'If we use a couple of those spears to widen that crack . . .' She redirected the torch beam to the vault ceiling. 'The roof'll come down and smash open the sarcophagus.'

'And what about us?'

Callie raised an eyebrow. 'I didn't say it was going to be risk-free . . .'

Nick grinned. 'Okay. Let's do it!' He stood up and chose a spear. It was a ceremonial weapon, made purely of bronze – much too heavy to fight with but perfect for destroying a three-thousand-year-old ceiling.

'As soon as it starts to cave in, get back into the passageway,' instructed Callie.

'I'll be in there so fast, all you'll see is a blur,' said Nick.

They both jammed a spear point into the gap between the ceiling blocks, and started working them back and forward like levers.

'Look, it's working,' exclaimed Nick, after only a few minutes' effort.

Callie followed Nick's gaze. One of the stone blocks was moving a little from side to side. Particles of dust were drizzling down. She pulled her own spear free and dug it into the gap Nick had made. There was a great cracking sound, and the whole block jolted towards them before they could move. It stopped, dangling precariously.

'Get into the passageway,' Callie ordered.

'Let me do it.'

'No, it's too dangerous.'

The block started to move again without any more help. Callie and Nick flung themselves into the passageway, Callie turning at the last minute to see blocks the size of microwave ovens falling right where they'd just been standing. There was a series of deafening crashes, and a wall of dust blasted into the passageway, making them both cough and splutter.

When everything had gone quiet again, Callie climbed out over the rubble.

Sunlight was flooding through a hole where the roof had been. At least half of the guardian lions had been smashed by tumbling blocks and right in the centre of the vault, the lion sarcophagus was broken in half! As the dust finished settling, Callie could see the third bronze key – grasped in the skeletal fingers of King Akanon's father.

'It looks like he's giving it to us,' coughed Nick.

Callie felt a ghostly chill as she detached the bronze key from the bony fingers. He had indeed handed it to her.

The key had the familiar lion-head moulding one end, and yet another arrangement of teeth the other. Callie placed it safely into her backpack and looked up at the opening.

A dog was barking. 'Skatelios!' shouted Nick. 'He's all right.' Skatelios was standing on the edge of the roof hole, wagging his tail.

'This way.' Callie pointed at one of the surviving lion statues. Its raking paw was like the first step of a ladder. She climbed onto the paw, and pulled herself up to its head. A second later, and she was out into the daylight.

18
HELICOPTER CHASE

If they headed north, away from Nekrotafio, they could cut off the entire south-west corner of Thelta. Then they could travel along the coast right back to their villa and King Akanon's Treasury.

Skatelios was barking again, and glowering at the sky.

When they heard the 'thrumb thrumb thrumb' of helicopter blades, it was too late. They were out in the open, and the crimson, shark-like helicopter had seen them. It was zeroing in, nose low, tail high.

'Now what do we do?' yelled Nick, starting to run.

'Keep on for the beach,' Callie screamed back, above the sound of the helicopter. 'Maybe there'll be a cave or some rocks where we can hide until it gets dark.'

And maybe there won't be a place where Skatelios can land and hunt us down on foot, she added to herself hopelessly.

Skatelios I rushed overhead, so low it barely cleared the ground. The air it disturbed hit them from behind like a tidal wave. It swung through a one hundred and eighty degree turn almost on the spot, and faced them. Skatelios was at the control column, and he was clearly a skilled pilot. Glass Eye was beside him in the cockpit, looking excited at the prospect of mowing them down. In his hands he held a rifle.

Skatelios rotated the helicopter another quarter turn, and Glass Eye brought the rifle to bear through the open cockpit door. Callie and Nick changed directions before he could squeeze the trigger.

Skatelios must have adjusted the helicopter in a micro-second, because it was hunting them down again almost instantly.

'DOWN!' Instinctively Callie flung herself to the ground as the helicopter made a lightning pass above their heads. It was even lower this time: barely a metre off the ground. The helicopter's skids, its ski-like feet, would have sliced them in half if they hadn't thrown themselves down.

Skatelios was forced to climb again to avoid a rocky outcrop, and it gave Callie and Nick vital seconds to make a last effort for the beach. But there was no way down! The hill had come to an abrupt end a distance above the beach. There was an overhang of crumbling orange soil and a steep slope to the sand.

Callie made a decision. If they slid down, Skatelios would find it impossible to come in close without carving the helicopter's rotors into the hillside.

A shot rang out, and Skatelios yelped at Nick's heels. He must have just *felt* the bullet zing past, because he ran on unharmed.

'Follow me!' Callie flung herself straight over the cliff without stopping, and was immediately sliding. Coarse grass and shrubs lacerated her skin, but the soil was loose, and helped her slide. Running on all fours, Skatelios managed to scurry halfway down the hill before rolling the rest of the way like an avalanche. He sprang to his paws again at the bottom. Callie and Nick landed behind him in a cloud of orange dust.

There were no caves, no rocks, and darkness was another hour away. All there were a few giant cactuses, punching out of the sand. The strip of beach was no wider than a footpath and they were trapped between the bottom of the cliff and the sea. Thankfully, there was nowhere for Skatelios to land.

Skatelios I fell out of the sky before them and hovered over the water. Skatelios swung the machine around so he could shout through his open cockpit door. His eyes were bulging and unblinking, his voice a scream through clenched teeth: 'GIVE...ME...THOSE...KEYS.'

'Callie, don't...' Nick stammered.

Callie shook her head at him, then slowly removed her backpack and started forward. If she gave Skatelios the keys, he would just spin the helicopter round and let Glass Eye shoot them. He had promised them nothing.

She climbed onto a low rock, to get closer to the nearside skid of the hovering helicopter. Out of the corner of her eye she could see one of the cactuses. She held the pink backpack in both hands and threw... It fell short, exactly as she'd intended. Skatelios automatically leaned out of the helicopter door to make a grab for it. As he did, his other hand jerked the control column to the left, pitching the helicopter onto its side. The rotor blades hacked through two of the giant cactuses at a stroke, like

212

a knife slicing through cucumber. Callie's backpack landed in the sand.

The helicopter staggered back, rocking and vibrating. There was a look of unimaginable hatred on Skatelios's face. The rotor blades must have been damaged – not fatally, but the helicopter seemed unable to climb and skittered sideways across the water with Skatelios fighting the control column.

'He's going! HE'S GOING!' shouted Nick triumphantly, as the helicopter staggered away along the coast making an unhealthy noise.

Callie could scarcely believe it. 'He's trying to save his helicopter before he takes his final revenge on us,' she said. 'He won't give up until he's killed us!'

She picked up her backpack, and scanned the horizon. The daylight was beginning to fade. It would soon be dark. 'Come on, Manolis,' she whispered, peering at the cobalt blue sea hopefully. 'You promised you'd help us.'

'Of course! Manolis!' Nick shouted.

'He's got to come,' said Callie. 'Else it's all over.'

As yet there was no small boat on the horizon tending the lobster pots. Suddenly Callie had a horrible feeling that Manolis only fished the coastal waters either side of his dad's taverna.

'He'll be here.' Nick was suddenly confident.

Callie couldn't think what they'd do if Manolis didn't come to rescue them. They'd never get back up that cliff, and how long would it be before Skatelios came back in his motorboat?

'I hope Manolis has got plenty of food,' Nick went on. 'Any minute now I'm going to start eating Skatelios.' The dog put its head on one side and whined.

'I don't know about food. I'm just tired,' said Callie.

Nick frowned thoughtfully and looked around. There was lots of dry grass at the bottom of the cliff. He started pulling it up in handfuls.

Maybe he was going to eat it, thought Callie vaguely. But he was laying it carefully over the soft sand in the lee of the rock. He wasn't satisfied until he'd brought three bundles of grass, and made a pillow out of his backpack. Then he was guiding her to the grass bed.

'Where's the torch to signal with?' he asked.

Callie hesitated.

'I won't fall asleep,' he promised seriously.

Callie gave him the torch and curled up on the grass. 'Thanks.' Sometimes she quite liked her brother.

She thought she was dreaming.

'Is she all right?' The concerned voice belonged to Manolis.

'Yeah! She's only sleeping.'

'Help me carry her to my boat.'

Callie dreamed she was being lifted by strong hands, and then she was gently rocking.

'When it got dark I didn't think you were going to come.' It was Nick's voice.

'I was needed at the taverna. There was damage caused by the earthquake.'

'Was anyone hurt?'

'By a miracle, no, and already my father has re-opened. He says even after an earthquake, people must eat.'

'Yep,' said Nick. 'I'm one of them.'

Manolis laughed. 'I have bread and cold meat, and even a little wine.'

'That's much better than eating Skatelios,' said Nick. Callie dreamed that a dog had barked. 'This is Skatelios by the way.'

'When did you become the owner of a dog, Niko?' asked Manolis.

'When Skatelios set it on us to rip us to pieces... He's quite friendly actually.'

Callie opened her eyes and yawned. She was on Manolis's little red and yellow fishing boat. Nick and Skatelios were wolfing down cold meat.

'I'll try some of that wine now,' said Nick.

'Oh no, you don't!' said Callie, sitting up, wide awake. Then she remembered how much Nick had grown up over the past few days. She felt ashamed of herself. 'Sorry, Nick. Have wine if you want, but I wouldn't tell Mum and Dad if I were you.'

Nick grinned and helped himself to half a cup of wine.

Manolis shared the rest of the food with Callie, and got his boat under way, heading north along the western coast of Thelta.

After they'd finished eating, they showed Manolis the three bronze keys.

'You have done what all Theltans have dreamed of

doing for over three thousand years,' breathed Manolis in awe. 'How have you achieved such a miracle?'

They told him the story attached to each bronze key. Manolis kept shaking his head in wonder and saying, 'No,' and, 'That must have been terrifying,' and once, 'I would have been too scared to even try.' He was so impressed with their bravery and ingenuity that Callie thought, Any minute now he's going to ask us for our autographs. He made her feel as if they'd done something really heroic, yet all they'd been trying to do was open King Akanon's Treasury, so they could save their parents.

She could see Nick was loving every minute of it. He kept remembering little details he'd forgotten to include on the first telling of the story, and remembering them in the wrong order. 'Yeah, and then he started firing a machine gun at us. A machine gun...! Callie was a complete mentalist – climbing right into the well before she even knew there'd be anything to hang onto... And when we got to the last place we couldn't see anything at all!'

'Manolis, what does the word *Nekrotafio* mean in Greek?' asked Callie.

Manolis replied without hesitation, 'Cemetery.'

'So that's it!' exclaimed Callie. 'The place where we found the last key was called Nekrotafio. It must have been known as a cemetery ever since Mycenaean times.'

'If it hadn't been for the earthquake, we'd never have found it,' added Nick.

'Was the earthquake bad on the rest of the island?' asked Callie.

'No, we had some warning of it on television and radio. Some older buildings were damaged, but no people were badly hurt. Everybody is talking about how lucky we have been.'

So have we, thought Callie. So far…

Manolis put his finger to his lips and pointed at Nick. He was curled up in the bottom of the boat with his arms around Skatelios. They were both fast asleep and Skatelios was making little doggy snoring noises.

Callie lowered her voice. 'Manolis, can me and Nick spend the night on your boat?'

'Of course, but the outhouse was not damaged in the earthquake. Why don't you sleep there? I told my father that it was you and Niko, the other night, and he said that if we had told him, he would have helped you.'

'Does he know about our arrangement – if we signal to you?'

'No.' Manolis shook his head guiltily. He clearly didn't like lying to his parents. 'I thought he might not let me make my normal trips, if he thought I was in danger. But you can trust my parents, Callie, they will not betray you to Georgiou Skatelios.'

Callie was sure Manolis was right. His parents were good people. The Skatelios they'd respected was a successful entrepreneur, not a gold-crazed maniac. She tried to explain, 'We've told you what Skatelios is capable of, Manolis. I don't want to put your parents in the same situation mine are in.' She gazed into his eyes. 'I already hate myself for making you take so many risks.'

'But, Callie, you are my friend.' Manolis reached out and took her hand. Callie didn't attempt to pull away. His touch was warm and comforting.

'Then please listen to me,' she said quietly. 'If we can get through this – me and Nick and our parents will be safely off the island, but you and your family won't be. If Skatelios finds out you've helped us, he'll get his own back on you. I know he will, and he has men working for him who hurt people for fun.'

'But—'

'It's no good arguing, Manolis, I won't change my mind.'

Manolis held her gaze for what seemed like an age, and then finally nodded. 'Then tell me how I *can* help you?'

19
GOLD CITY

Callie and Nick spent the night on Manolis's boat, warm under a thick tarpaulin. At first light Manolis climbed back on board with far more food than he would normally bring for his own breakfast. He pulled the cord to bring the outboard motor buzzing into action, and aimed the boat across the turquoise shallows. As soon as they rounded the headland, and no more houses were in sight, he flipped back the tarpaulin.

'*Kalimera.*'

'Good morning,' Callie and Nick said together.

Nick took charge of the breakfast, and Skatelios's long, pointed snout disappeared straight into the waterproof container. 'Hey, where's the wine?' Nick asked disappointedly.

Manolis smiled and handed Callie her mobile phone. 'Fully charged,' he reported. Callie nodded gravely. She would need it to call Andreas.

'Now you have to check your lobster pots as usual,' she told him. 'You mustn't do anything you don't normally do, so when you reach Limani Bay, we'll swim ashore.'

Everyone, including Skatelios, looked astonished. Callie was volunteering to swim.

'I can take you in—' began Manolis.

'No,' Callie cut him off firmly. 'Skatelios Island is right

in front of the bay. If you're seen going into shore they're bound to be suspicious.'

Manolis must have thought she was right, because he offered no further argument. 'What about the dog?' he asked instead.

Nick looked up from his breakfast of *tyropitakia,* a delicious cheese pie. 'What about him?'

Callie hadn't stopped to think about Skatelios. 'Will you take him for us, Manolis?'

'Why can't he come with us?' demanded Nick.

'He'll slow us down, and Andreas won't have made arrangements for him.'

Nick was silent for a minute, and then, surprisingly, just ruffled Skatelios's pointed black ears and said, 'Sorry, boy.'

Callie turned back to Manolis. 'I don't think his real owner will come looking for him, but for goodness sake give him a different name.'

'Rover?' said Manolis, choosing a very English-sounding dog's name.

It was another thirty minutes before they sailed into the bay beneath Villa Limani and opposite Skatelios Island, time enough for them to slip back under the tarpaulin. Callie was sure Manolis had brought his boat in closer to shore than usual, but if anyone were watching, it would look normal enough as he dropped a weighted lobster pot secured to a marker buoy over the side.

'Okay,' whispered Manolis. He knelt in the middle of the boat to fold the tarpaulin, while Callie and Nick slid over the side behind him and hidden from view. There was a third splash. Skatelios, it seemed, had not agreed to another change of ownership.

Manolis continued folding the tarpaulin until they were almost halfway to the shore. Then Callie saw that he was guiding his boat on an angle to keep them hidden from Skatelios Island for as long as possible.

Barely moments after Manolis's boat disappeared from view, Callie and Nick swam round a rocky outcrop. They staggered out onto the concrete-like beach, and Skatelios paddled out after them. He shook himself like a lawn sprinkler and started to wag his tail at Nick.

'Good boy,' said Nick, and gave Callie a slightly apologetic look.

'Well, *I* never thought he'd stay behind...'

'I thought you gave up easily,' admitted Callie. She should have got Manolis to tie Skatelios up.

'Anyway, we might need him,' added Nick.

'Yes, because if *we* can't unlock the Treasury door – *he'll* obviously be able to do it with his little doggy paws, won't he?' said Callie with sarcasm. Skatelios put his head on one side and gave her a puzzled look. She sighed with resignation and patted him on the head.

'Come on, we can't hang around here. Someone might come down from the village and raise the alarm, seeing as how we're on the police's Most Wanted list!'

They hurried up the mud road, past the familiar cactuses and the wild-growing oregano, ready to dive into the bushes at the slightest sign of locals. Keeping low, they made it as far as the boundary wall of Villa Limani without seeing anyone.

'Round the back,' whispered Callie. Instead of going in at the concrete driveway, she dashed straight past, and dobbed down into a drainage channel on the outside of the wall. Skatelios loped along beside them, his great pink tongue lolling out of the side of his mouth.

Nick peered over the wall. 'It doesn't look like the villa was damaged in the earthquake.'

Callie gaped at him in surprise. 'What are you talking about?' The back wall of the villa had a long jagged crack running right the way from the roof to the ground. And somebody had boarded up the patio doors.

'Skatelios probably did that with our jeep!'

'Maybe,' said Callie. She just hoped the whole place wasn't about to come crashing down with them in it.

Skatelios was making a low, rumbling growl.

'What's the matter with hi—'

'Get down!' Callie hissed urgently. Lobster Tan Man had just wandered out of their villa.

Nick spotted him too. 'What's he doing here?' he hissed.

'Skatelios! Either Mum and Dad have told him, or he's worked it out: King Akanon's Treasury is here. We were bound to come back once we had all three keys, and Lobster Tan is lying in wait for us.'

'What's he doing now?'

Callie risked a look. Lobster Tan was waddling down the mud road with a blue towel over his shoulder. 'I think he's going to the beach to work on his tan.'

Nick looked over the top of the wall. 'He's got one of our towels!'

'Come on, we might not have long before he comes back.'

Lobster Tan had left the side door of the villa on the latch. Callie opened it, and felt as if she was going to be sick as they went inside. The last time they'd walked through that door they had been with Mum and Dad.

The lounge was darker than usual because of the boards across the wrecked patio doors. What light there was, was filtering in through the side door and two windows. Everything else was as Callie remembered it – the smashed glass had been swept up and all the furniture had been returned to its normal position. It was disgusting, thinking that Lobster Tan had been touching all their stuff.

'Where do we start?' asked Nick. 'Mum and Dad wouldn't tell you *how* they got under the villa.'

'I've been thinking about that,' replied Callie. 'You remember the night we couldn't find them?'

Nick nodded. 'Yep.'

'And we couldn't sleep after...? Well, I'd swear I never heard them come back in.'

Nick was shaking his head. 'Neither did I, but they must have done – they were here at breakfast.'

'What I mean is, maybe they never left at all.'

Nick's eyes widened as he realised what she was getting at. 'There's a secret trap door or something.'

223

'It's the only way I can explain why I didn't hear the outside door.'

Nick scanned the lounge as if looking for a door he'd never noticed before. 'Where then?'

'The cellar. It's the lowest part of the villa, and Dad said the Treasury was underground...'

The cellar was still a total mess. The steel shelving units and trays of pottery fragments they'd contained were exactly how they'd left them, strewn all over the floor. Callie squatted down to look for signs of a trap door. Skatelios seemed to think it was a game and kept getting in her way. 'Go away, Skatelios!'

Skatelios licked her face.

'I can't see a thing,' Callie admitted, after running her hands all over the tiled floor. She sat up and caught her reflection in the full-length mirror. She looked *awful*! Her hair was a tangled mess, her clothes looked as if she'd found them in a dustbin, and her skin was nearly as red as Lobster Tan Man's!

'And this is helping us how?' Nick asked her reflection.

Callie continued to stare into the mirror, frowning. 'I've always wondered why they brought that thing into the cellar,' she said. 'What are they doing down here – getting ready to go out or what?'

'Maybe they are!' exclaimed Nick.

They started dragging the fallen shelf units out of the way to examine the mirror.

'I wish I'd still got my sword,' Nick said, when they were able to stand right in front of the mirror.

Callie shook her head. 'No. What use would it be if they had to smash it every time they went through? It must open.' She felt carefully around the edge of the mirror and tried to slide it along. It wouldn't budge.

'Try pulling it.'

There was a slight, but perceptible click, and the mirror swung open on hinges. It was a door! Behind it plaster and breeze block had been chiselled away. There was a short tunnel through soil and then a room – a far older, far finer room than any that belonged to the villa. It was from a Mycenaean building, and at the end of it were some three-thousand-year-old steps. The villa builders had missed the entrance to King Akanon's Treasury by only metres!

'It must have taken Mum and Dad ages to dig all the way through that,' said Nick, staring at the breeze blocks and soil.

'I bet they came down here whenever we were out,' Callie guessed. 'And then they were so close to getting the completed map, they came down to finish it off that night.'

A distinct slamming sound caught both their attentions. Callie immediately knew what it was. 'Lobster Tan's back!'

They held their breaths, listening intently. Lobster Tan was moving about upstairs. After a minute they heard the television.

Skatelios barked.

It went quiet again upstairs.

Callie hurtled up the cellar steps and threw herself at

the light switch, then flew back down by the light of Manolis's torch. 'Quick! Behind the mirror!' she hissed.

Callie closed the mirror door seconds before they heard Lobster Tan coming into the cellar. He walked down the steps and his shoes crunched on pieces of broken pottery. Callie had her hands locked tightly around Skatelios's muzzle. After an agonising wait, they heard the cellar door close again. Skatelios was licking Callie's fingers, and she started to breathe again. Distantly, she heard the television going on again. She rolled her eyes at Nick.

The torch beam flickered off the wall. It was glazed with small oblong tiles the colour of the midnight sky. They started to descend the Mycenaean steps, walking through a stone gateway, with a bronze lion on either side. They carried on into a giant chamber, undecorated and unadorned, just sandstone block walls reaching ten metres high, and in the middle of them, surely the largest bronze doors in the world. They met down the middle, and the right hand door had three keyholes cut into it, one on top of the other.

Callie recognised everything from her dreams and wondered uncomfortably how she could possibly have known.

Nick stood aghast in front of the vast doors.

Callie found a small, oil-powered light generator. 'Mum and Dad must've brought this down.' She started it up the way she'd seen her dad doing on underground digs before. The round searchlight flooded every corner of the chamber with shimmering white light.

Nick blinked for a second in the glare, and then put his eye up to one of the keyholes.

'Well?' demanded Callie impatiently.

'I can't see a thing.'

Callie could feel butterflies in her stomach, and the palms of her hands were sweating as she pulled the three bronze keys out of her backpack.

'What if it's empty?' asked Nick suddenly.

'DON'T! For goodness sake, DON'T!' Callie took a deep breath and slid the first key into the first hole. It didn't go in all the way. She tried it in the second hole. Again, it didn't fit properly. With a shaking hand, she tried it in the last keyhole. The key disappeared, right up to its lion-head handle. Callie sighed with relief. The second key was easier. She chose correctly first time and it went straight home in the topmost keyhole. That only left one key and one keyhole. Callie slowly slid the final key into the final keyhole. It stopped: sticking out at least two centimetres further than the other two, and feeling loose. She tried to turn it where it was, but it wouldn't budge. She stared at Nick, who had gone deathly pale. She could hear him swallowing a lump in his throat.

Callie was gripped by a sudden panic. What if one of the keys they'd collected was a false key? Then what would they do? Would they have to start all over again? Callie tried to quell the panic and took another deep breath. She turned the top key clockwise. There was a reassuring click, loud enough to have been made by a key five times as big. Callie reached for the bottom key and turned it. Another comfortingly loud click. She reinserted the middle key. This time it went all the way home. Nick patted her on the back. Callie turned the key. It made the same loud clicking noise as the two before it and a great whirring sound filled the entrance chamber. The immense doors began to swing slowly outward a millimetre at a time. Beyond them they could see two heavy counterweights lowering gradually to the ground, and a pulley system dragging the doors apart. Callie redirected the beam from the light generator between the bronze doors.

NOTHING could have prepared her for what lay inside.

It was a room of gold, of splendour and of opulence. It was bigger than Callie's school assembly hall, with a panelled roof supported by a forest of marble pillars. A colonnaded aisle surged up to a magnificent balcony flanked by two winged lions five metres high and made of gold. The floor was a sea of turquoise tiles interrupted by colourful patterns representing turtles and dolphins and a giant squid.

'I bet Mum and Dad wish they were here,' croaked Callie.

'I bet they wish they were *anywhere*,' replied Nick.

The entrance was filled with gigantic urns, many rows deep, and they were brimming with gold coin. Standing before the wall on one side were golden statues of gods and goddesses; of animals including jackals, lions and antelope, vultures, eagles and horses. In front of the other wall was piled golden armour, shields and breastplates, swords and spears – so numerous they were stacked half way to the ceiling. The weaponry was of such quality, no archaeologist could ever have seen its equal.

Under the winged-lion balcony stood a dazzling war chariot, too heavy with gold and jewels to be pulled by any ordinary horse, such fine harnesses had been built for what must have been animals of monster-like proportions. On the balcony itself, like a setting sun, was a gigantic face with blue tiled eyes and ruby encrusted lips, with wavy strips of white gold to represent flowing hair. Its sapphire gaze fell upon an offering pool, encircled by gold bricks and with deep black water.

Callie could find no words. She could barely find her breath. This was wealth beyond wealth, riches beyond riches: the ancient treasure of Thelta.

'It's gold city!' said Nick, more simply, taking up a double handful of gold coins.

Callie nodded. It was Gold City. It was almost too much to behold, as if she might go blind just by daring to look on such splendour. In just one blink she could see more treasure than she had ever imagined.

'How did they get it all down here?' asked Nick, standing on the platform of the war chariot.

'They must have built most of it in here,' replied Callie. 'There must have been craftsmen working for years.'

'Better than a piggy bank, isn't it?'

Callie grinned and looked around again. Her gaze fell upon the golden mask on the balcony: King Akanon without a doubt, flawless youthful beauty, and unbearded. She was offering him silent thanks. It was a king's ransom, and every gold kilogram of it was insignificant when weighed against the lives of her parents...

She removed her mobile phone from its protective plastic bag and pressed the call key for Andreas. It rang several times before she heard a man identifying himself.

'Andreas.'

Lying next to a jackal statue, Skatelios gave a low, throaty growl.

'It's Callie Latham, and I'm standing in King Akanon's Treasury.'

'Is it...?'

'It's more incredible than you could ever dream.'

There was a pause. Callie wasn't surprised. It had all seemed impossible and yet here they were.

Andreas's voice came again. 'How did you get in there?'

Callie quickly told him about the mirror in the cellar, and then added, 'One of your father's men is hanging about. You'll have to get past him.'

'Very well, stay where you are. You and your family will be reunited before midnight. Do you understand?'

Callie nodded. 'Yes, I understand.' She rang off.

'He's bringing Mum and Dad,' she said faintly. When she saw them again she would finally allow herself to stop worrying.

20

SINK OR SWIM

Ten minutes later and they'd eaten the rest of the bread and cold meat which Manolis had given them that morning, and had wandered around touching all the beautiful objects of treasure. Skatelios had lifted his leg and urinated on the golden jackal.

'What do you think Andreas will do with it all?' asked Nick.

Callie thought about the sheer enormity of the treasure. 'He won't be able to go home after he's helped Mum and Dad escape... He'll probably take whatever he can load onto his boat – the smaller stuff like the coins and maybe one of the statues.'

'He'll probably sink then,' said Nick.

'If he takes the keys with him nobody can touch the rest, and he'll be able to come back one day after his father's gone,' Callie added. She didn't mind Andreas taking the treasure any more. He'd saved their lives at the river and was about to save their parents.

A bloodcurdling scream twisted Callie round on her feet.

Inconceivably, Georgiou Skatelios was standing just inside the great bronze doors, flanked by Glass Eye and Lobster Tan Man. He screamed again and fell to his knees with his arms outstretched towards the heavens, his face distorted between torture and ecstasy. His eyes looked bulbous, as if they might explode from his skull at the sight of so much gold. Saliva was bubbling out from between his lips.

'GET THEM OUT!' he yelled, neither looking at Callie and Nick, nor Glass Eye and Lobster Tan, his gaze fixed maniacally on the huge golden mask of King Akanon. 'GET THEM OUT!'

Glass Eye dragged Callie and Nick roughly through the parted Treasury doors. Skatelios's own dog was snarling viciously, but Lobster Tan managed to avoid his snapping jaws, and haul him away with them. The last view Callie saw of the Treasury was Skatelios with his fingers digging into his own skull, and the last sound she heard was his low gurgling murmur.

Glass Eye shoved her and Nick onto the steps outside the bronze-lion gateway, while Lobster Tan sent a yelping Skatelios in their direction with a kick. 'It seems that Andreas wasn't the only one of Mr Skatelios's dogs you managed to bring to heel.'

Skatelios growled threateningly.

'I see you survived your snakebite,' sneered Callie. 'What happened? Did the snake die?'

Glass Eye started to laugh loudly.

Lobster Tan ignored him. 'Not quite who you were expecting, are we? I'm afraid Andreas met with a rather unfortunate, and rather extreme, accident... A hit-and-run driver by all accounts.'

Glass Eye took a sickening bow, and mimed steering a

232

car. 'You next. This time no crowd.' He rolled just one of his eyes.

'It was patently obvious Mr Skatelios couldn't trust Andreas anymore, after you two slipped past him at the river.'

Callie felt ill. Skatelios had had his own son killed! She suddenly realised she must have been speaking to Skatelios, not Andreas, on her mobile phone. He had even used his catchphrase: Do you understand?

'None of it will do him any good,' she said defiantly, 'The treasure's too massive to remove.'

'Haven't you heard? Your father signed over Villa Limani to Mr Skatelios this morning. He's going to turn it into his own private museum, to go along with the one on his island.'

Callie stared at Lobster Tan. Her dad would never have signed the villa over willingly.

'It's all quite legal.' Lobster Tan interpreted her expression. 'Mr Skatelios even deposited four hundred thousand euros into your father's bank account, in case anyone asked questions.'

'He's let Mum and Dad go?' demanded Nick, a ray of hope in his eyes.

'Let them go?' scoffed Lobster Tan. 'What planet are *you* on?'

'Skatelios has "special" plan for parents,' Glass Eye said, with a malicious smile. 'Very special.'

'Shame you won't be around to enjoy it,' Lobster Tan added.

He and Glass Eye grinned at each other and Lobster Tan started going through Callie's backpack.

'Mr Skatelios will be very pleased to have these in his museum,' he said, removing the four clay tablets which had been the cause of so much misery. 'I may even get the extra pocket money he promised me after all.' He leered at Callie. 'You could have saved yourself a lot of extra effort if you hadn't kept dashing off.'

'Dashing!' exclaimed Nick contemptuously. 'We didn't need to *dash* with someone as fat as you chasing us.'

Lobster Tan rewarded Nick by kicking his feet. Skatelios growled. Lobster Tan carried on looking through Callie's backpack. 'The latest mobile. I've been wanting to get my hands on one of these. Any credit on it?' He started playing with the phone as if it had been his all along.

'What's this?' He stuck the mobile phone under Callie's nose. It was displaying one of the photographs of King Akanon and Princess Electra she'd taken in the tomb at Nekrotafio.

'Haven't you heard?' Callie copied his own phrase. 'That's King Akanon and Princess Electra. I don't think your master will be quite so pleased about that, though.'

'Yeah, because we smashed it into pieces,' Nick joined in. 'Tiny pieces.'

Lobster Tan pocketed the mobile phone and kicked Nick's feet again. Skatelios snapped at him.

They seemed to be sitting there for hours before Skatelios finally reappeared from the Treasury. His face

234

was contorted with insanity. 'LOCK THEM INSIDE! King Akanon demands their deaths...Bring the dog.'

Callie found herself landing on the glazed Treasury floor with a bump. Nick landed right beside her. Slowly, the thick bronze doors began to close behind them. They heard Skatelios barking frantically, and saw the strip of light become a thread and then blackness. A final, shuddering thud and they were trapped for good. Callie felt in the pocket of her shorts. Her fingers closed comfortingly around Manolis's torch. She switched it on and wondered how long the batteries would last.

'What was that?'

Callie looked round. 'What was what?'

Nick was staring up at the Treasury's panelled ceiling.

'I thought I heard something up there.'

'I didn't hear anything.' Callie aimed the torch beam. She could see flecks of dust drizzling through the light. Then she heard the noise too. It sounded as if two stone blocks were scraping against each other. Was the ceiling *MOVING*? Callie swallowed a lump in her throat. That could only mean...

'You know I said King Akanon had had the Treasury built so it would collapse if anyone tried to break in?'

'Y – e – s...?'

Callie hadn't taken her gaze off the ceiling. 'Well, I think someone's trying to break in.'

'Who?'

'I don't know...Maybe Lobster Tan or Glass Eye have

come back to steal some gold for themselves. DOES IT MATTER?'

She ran desperately to the bronze doors and listened. She couldn't hear a thing through them; they were half a metre thick!

'STOP! STOP!' she yelled. 'YOU'LL DESTROY IT ALL.'

'And us,' added Nick, swallowing.

All they heard in reply was another crunching sound directly above them.

Callie swept the torch around wildly. They had to get out of here. NOW! But the Treasury was a plain oblong, with no way in or out but the bronze doors. There was nothing! No escape.

Callie prayed to King Akanon's gods to help her.

The torch beam reflected off the water in the small round offering pool. Callie stared at it in surprise. 'What's water doing here after three thousand years? It should have evaporated.' She cupped her hand to taste it.

'What?' Nick asked.

'It's salt water!'

'Right. Good. Which means?' He glanced nervously at the ceiling.

Callie was trying to work it out. She pointed the torch into the water. STEPS! She could see steps fanning out. 'It's a spiral staircase. Look!'

Nick leaned over the edge. 'Under water? Who for? Mycenaean mermaids?'

Callie worked it out at a rush: 'It's not meant to be

236

underwater. It's flooded! We must be right next to the sea, or even *under* it.'

Nick shook his head. 'Wait. Why would they go to all the trouble of hiding the keys in impossible places, if there was a back door?'

'It wasn't a back door. Not then.'

Nick broke into a smile. 'The earthquake! It's made another way out!'

Another scraping sound came from the ceiling. Callie stared into the water, an unpleasant feeling in the pit of her stomach. She couldn't be asked to dive underwater. She just couldn't! It was like voluntarily drowning. And this wouldn't be like her head momentarily going under a wave. She would have to swim downwards. And how far was it to the bottom? What was there? Another chamber? That had to be flooded too, or the seawater would never have got this far. COULD THEY GET OUT? Callie wanted to scream.

She flicked the torch beam onto the ceiling. Did it look *lower?*

She stepped into the water and immediately recoiled at the iciness of it. 'It's freezing cold!' It was going to be the coldest water she'd ever swum in. She took another step, reacting again to the shock, as the water rose higher up her legs. One at a time she took three more icy steps until the water reached her waist.

'Splash your arms and body before you go any further,' advised Nick. 'It'll help you acclimatise to it.'

Callie took his advice, shivering, and then took four

more steps until only her head and shoulders remained above the water. Panic reasserted itself: she was about to go deep under the water, without even knowing where she was going; a rumble from the ceiling reminded her why.

Manolis's torch was right below the water now. The beam still worked and she could see another dozen steps further down, before the light dissolved into blackness. She looked up at Nick: the merest dark shadow, now that the torch was pointed away from him.

'You can do it, Callie. I know you can do it.'

Callie smiled faintly, and took a deep breath. She dived. Water filled her eyes, and nose, and ears unpleasantly. Then she was swimming downwards.

It was unexpectedly difficult to swim down, almost as if the water wanted to carry her safely back towards oxygen. The breaststroke motion of her arms was sweeping the torch from side to side erratically, and she still couldn't see the bottom of the spiral staircase. She swam on. And on.

She wasn't sure how long she'd been swimming, but suddenly, quite suddenly, she was right out of air. For a second, she thought about carrying on. She might be closer to air in front of her than behind, but there was no way of knowing. She had to go back. *She had to go back.* She swung around clumsily in the water and was shocked to find Nick right behind her. He understood immediately and turned with her.

Callie fought upwards for several more metres. Her chest felt as if it were being crushed and she was losing coordination in her arms and legs. Darkness began to close around her. Why was it getting so dark? Then she realised. She'd dropped the torch, and vaguely, she could see it sinking beneath her.

How much further? She was blacking out! Then strong arms were propelling her forward, not hers, but Nick's, and she was spluttering and gasping – heaving oxygen into her lungs again. She couldn't see him, but she could hear Nick gasping beside her.

Callie dragged herself out of the water-filled staircase and onto the Treasury floor. She lay there half dead. They had two choices before them: be crushed by the Treasury roof, or drown.

She heard a tiny, but frightening 'clang'. Part of the ceiling must have fallen and pinged off something gold. Callie wished she could see the ceiling. Why had she had to drop the torch? It had probably sunk right to the bottom of the staircase.

In the pitch darkness, she smiled faintly.

'I think I've got an idea.'

'About time too!' said Nick hoarsely. 'What is it?'

'If we hold onto something heavy we'll sink without having to swim. We can drop straight to the bottom and still have most of our breath to either go straight on or swim back up.'

'Brilliant!' She heard excitement in Nick's voice.

'We need some gold,' Callie went on.

They found it by groping around in the dark – a set of thick discs with holes in the centre, the size of small wheels. They could barely manage to roll one each back to the water.

Another lump of ceiling hit the floor beside Callie, as she stepped back into the seawater. 'Keep to the middle this time. It's like an empty shaft,' she said, walking down the first few steps.

She filled her lungs with air and plunged into the centre of the staircase. The last thing she heard was a thunderous crash, as if a block the size of a car had just dropped into the Treasury. Had Nick got into the water in time?

Callie sank like a brick. She counted the seconds: one second to every two beats of her heart. Ten seconds – twenty beats of her heart. Fifteen seconds – thirty beats of her heart. Then, light. Manolis's torch! Had it gone all the way to the bottom, or had it lodged somewhere halfway up? Four heartbeats later, Callie reached the torch. It was lying on a paved area in front of a wide archway. She dropped the gold disc and snatched up the torch instead. She jerked it upwards. Thankfully, Nick was sinking through the water in front of her.

Callie swam through the opening.

It was a chamber also flooded with sea water. A ten-metre high golden King Akanon stood watch over an underwater ship. Not one part of it wasn't made from gold or gems. Even the two great eyes either side of the battering ram of a prow were finished in a mosaic of diamonds and sapphires. It was the greatest single treasure in the entire Treasury, and Callie couldn't spare another second's look.

She swung the ghostly torch beam onto the painted-plaster wall and immediately saw a rift. There was no going back. Without a second's hesitation she swam on. Nick was already beside her.

The rift was wide enough to slip through easily. Instinctively Callie swam upwards, her chest beginning to feel as it had before – as though it was about to burst. On the verge of blackout, she told herself, 'Don't drop it this time. Don't drop the torch.' And then, inconceivably, a voice inside her head was saying: 'Switch it off!'

She did, and suddenly she could see dim blue water ahead, suffused with strawberry pink. She aimed for it. One last effort. Her fingertips clawed the jagged rock either side of her for purchase. Then the colours lightened in front of her, and she was right through the rift and swimming over yellow sand, the grains swirling around her like mist. Two seconds later and her head was above water her lungs refilling with huge gulps of air. It took her a moment to realise she was on her own.

'Nick...? NICK!'

21
MONSTER

Callie dived straight back under the water and swam back the way she'd come. She was swimming more strongly than ever before, with long, powerful strokes, diving towards the seabed still hazy with swirling sand. There was no sign of Nick, but *something* was stirring up the sand. She swam into the underwater cloud, sand grains stinging her eyes, and there he was.

His foot was caught in the rift, right where it narrowed away to almost nothing. He was struggling frantically with terror in his eyes. Callie locked an arm around his chest and heaved. He didn't move. She released her grip and dived down to his feet. One foot was completely trapped. She started working at it, clawing away pieces of sea bed with her fingernails. The seconds ticked away. Nick's struggles were becoming weaker. She dragged at his leg, and it released. Then he was free and they were both kicking for the pink-blue light.

They broke the water surface together.

It took several moments for Nick to recover his voice. 'I think you just saved my life.'

Callie grinned. 'We all make mistakes.'

Nick grinned back.

They weren't far from the shore. The only question was: which shore? It looked familiar, but if it was Limani

Bay, it was facing in the wrong direction.

'It's Skatelios Island,' Callie managed to say. 'We're right in front of it.'

'Mum and Dad!' was Nick's response.

Callie nodded and she started to swim again. All the way to the island, she was thinking about the inhuman cry they'd heard four nights ago. Did Skatelios own some kind of lion that roamed free on the island?

It was starting to get dark as they waded out of the water. A cold wind made Callie shiver in her wet clothes. She looked around and saw a mud and sand path leading away from the beach. She was sure it would bring them to Skatelios's mansion, which must be on the other side of the island. Since the start of the holiday she'd seen boats curving around the coast in that direction.

'Skatelios's villa?' asked Nick.

'Let's try it and see.'

They followed the path right to the top of a hill, and could see the rest of the island, lit up spectacularly in front of them. Skatelios's quayside was almost as impressive as the boat docks in Thelta Town. *Skatelios IV,* a three-deck cruiser, like a luxury hotel on water, had its own berth, while Skatelios's hire fleet, including cabin cruisers, two yachts, and a catamaran were all anchored at further jetties.

The red helicopter, with injured rotor blades removed, was standing on its own circular helipad. Skatelios had nursed it home.

'He so needs a billion more pounds in gold,' said Nick.

'There might not be any gold now – if the Treasury roof collapsed...'

'It did collapse! It only just missed me,' said Nick.

'All those beautiful treasures, lost forever. Skatelios kidnapped Mum and Dad, and killed his own son for *nothing*.'

A low, distant rumble made them both look up. The clouds had grown thicker and blacker. There was going to be a storm.

Further along the track, surrounded by cypress and pine trees, they saw Skatelios's *Megaron*. Four sweeping balconies, one atop the next, were set back along a slope like steps. Either side of it was a two-storey wing as long as a row of houses. The entire complex was pristine white, with scarlet shutters at the windows and black railings around the balconies; the roof was terracotta red. It was truly palatial. No palace in Mycenaean Greece could have been more spectacular, and it was all lit up like an electric light factory.

'Doesn't look like there's any earthquake damage,' said Nick, with a note of disappointment.

'Manolis said Thelta got away lightly. Only some of the older buildings were damaged,' Callie reminded him.

'Where is everyone?' frowned Nick. 'The whole island seems completely deserted. There's got to be more people than Lobster Tan and Glass Eye working for him. Where are all his servants?'

Nick was right. Callie hadn't seen anyone at the boat docks or the helipad either. There was no sign of life anywhere!

'I suppose he could have given everyone the night off,' suggested Nick.

Callie chewed her lip. 'Maybe he doesn't want anyone to see what he's planning to do with Mum and Dad…'

Nick glared at Skatelios's mansion. 'And how are we going to find them in *that*?'

Callie had no idea. 'I don't know. Let's find a way in first.'

They started at the end of the nearest wing. There was light spilling through the windows onto a cropped, well-cared-for lawn. Few of the windows were curtained, and they were able to peer right inside. The entire wing appeared to be servant or staff accommodation, and the rooms for the most part were bedrooms: furnished plainly. Still there was no sign of life.

They looked through a window into a canteen. It was utterly deserted.

'It's – *eerie*,' said Callie.

'Think what it'd be like if everyone was here though,' said Nick.

Callie realised he was right. 'We wouldn't stand a chance.'

They reached a little entranceway, halfway along the wing. Callie tried the door and it opened.

'They won't be in this bit,' said Nick. 'It's obviously the staff quarters. It'd be too dangerous.'

'Maybe,' agreed Callie, 'but we might be able to get into the main building this way.'

Nick nodded, 'Okay,' and they went inside.

The next few rooms were a TV lounge, some toilets and a games room, every one of them as empty as the rest of the wing.

Callie was beginning to relax when she heard a familiar sound further down the corridor. Someone was here. Someone had left a television on! It was another bedroom, and the door was propped open, giving them a view of everything inside. Unlike the bedrooms before, there were some nice things here – the TV was a plasma screen, plus there was a stereo system and better furniture. Without going in, Callie could see that no one was home.

She was suddenly dragged backwards. Somebody had a fistful of her hair. She managed to twist around, and *gagged*.

It was a face more terrifying than any she'd seen before. It was the face of death.

'*Lion Tattoo!*' she gasped.

His gaze was boring into her.

He'd escaped from the motorboat explosion after all, but just barely. His hair had been burnt away and his face was blistered and red. What remained of his lips were swelled and weeping, his breathing was restricted, rasping from a wasted nose. Callie recoiled from his lash-less, hate-filled eyes. He tried to swear at her but it was a voice that rattled rather than spoke.

Lion Tattoo wasn't expecting her to resist, and Callie jerked free from his grip, leaving him with a handful of her own hair. Nick tore past him at the same moment, and they both charged down the corridor. Lion Tattoo was faster on his feet than his burnt body suggested. Callie had covered no more than a few paces when he rugby-tackled her from behind, gripping her legs.

She clattered to the hard corridor floor, crying out as a spike of pain shot up from her right elbow.

Lion Tattoo held her down with his own vile body. He wheezed something into her ear, and Callie could feel his hot breath on the back of her neck.

'Hey! Lion Tattoo! Get off my sister!'

Callie turned her head to see Nick brandishing a crimson fire-extinguisher. He aimed the nozzle into Lion Tattoo's face and squeezed the trigger. Powder spurted into the blistered face. The scream echoed along the corridor, and Lion Tattoo rolled off Callie, clawing at his eyes.

Callie was immediately on her feet and running after Nick.

They sprinted down the rest of the corridor and through a door at the end. It was a shower room and the only way out was a narrow, horizontal window. Callie released the catch and flung it open. If they could squeeze through, Lion Tattoo's broader frame would never fit.

'Go first!' she shouted at Nick, and half helped him, half launched him through the window. She jumped up straight after him and was wriggling through when she heard the door slam open behind her.

Callie screamed. Lion Tattoo was hauling her back in by her legs. 'Nick!'

Nick grabbed her hands and started pulling her from outside. Lion Tattoo was winning! Terror made Callie lash out, and she felt her foot crunch into Lion Tattoo's mangled face. She saw him slither to the floor and not get up again.

She clawed the rest of the way out, pulling every muscle in her body, and dropped to the ground outside.

'I think I've knocked him out,' she panted. Nick blew out his cheeks in relief. His hands were shaking. Callie stood catching her breath.

For a moment, they were standing in the blazing electric light illuminating the mansion. Then, startlingly, the entire building was plunged into blackness. The security lights all around the mansion, inside the rooms, the jetty lights, and the helipad lights went out as if one giant switch had been thrown. Callie could barely make out the walls of the mansion right in front of her, the rest of the island had virtually disappeared.

She groped her way forward.

As her eyes adjusted to the dark, she could see they were on a path leading between the jetties in one direction, and further up the hill in the other. Flaming torches had been placed at intervals, and stretched all the way up the slope to a small, cliff-fringed plateau, perched on the side of the island. There, silhouetted against the clouds, were the columns of a Greek temple.

'Callie!' whispered Nick. He pointed towards the dark

shape of Skatelios's mansion. A door had opened only a few paces in front of them.

Callie pulled Nick behind some bushes and watched.

Three figures, dressed in white robes, had turned towards the temple, and were walking in a slow procession up the torch-lit path. In the flickering flame light, Callie could make out the faces of Skatelios, Glass Eye and Lobster Tan Man. It was some sort of sick ceremony. Now Callie *knew* how Skatelios was planning to deal with her parents. He was going to sacrifice them to the gods.

The three chilling figures were drawing away. Callie gave a little tug on Nick's T-shirt. They should follow them.

The wind was whipping up the torch flames, as they trailed the procession. Callie kept to the shadows at the side of the path, stumbling over uneven rocks. At last Skatelios stopped in front of the temple.

Callie could see every detail in the torchlight. Steps led to a paved area, where six, soaring columns supported a roof pediment, like a flattened triangle. It was decorated with scenes from the sea – not ancient scenes, but of Skatelios's own fleet with the three-decked cruiser, *Skatelios IV,* taking pride of place. In front of the temple was a large statue of Skatelios himself.

'He's totally barking,' whispered Nick. 'He's had this whole place built as if he really is King Akanon's heir.'

Callie crouched behind the low temple wall. 'He must have found out the island used to be part of King

Akanon's citadel,' she whispered. 'I bet the jetties, Skatelios's mansion and the temple have all been built on top of King Akanon's original sites.'

'What about the helicopter pad?' Nick whispered.

'I bet there was *something* Mycenaean there. Remember the winged lions? Maybe there was something like that there.'

Skatelios was scattering crimson rose petals while Lobster Tan and Glass Eye lit more torches. After a moment they started to move into the temple.

Callie worked her way along the wall until she could see into the temple. There was a warm orange glow from oil lamps, lighting up a marble-pillared hall. All three men had disappeared inside. 'Come on.' She had to see inside. She had to know if her mum and dad were in there.

They climbed over the wall and ran up the white stone steps. Pausing only a second, they made it through the middle of the six columns and came out onto a flawless marble floor. The temple was a long, wide corridor of pillars with semicircular alcoves on each side containing more statues of Skatelios!

'Not that he's in love with himself or anything,' said Nick.

'Where have they gone?' whispered Callie. There was no sign of Skatelios or his men.

There was a thud like the sound of a closing door. Callie tensed, but the sound had come from the other end of the temple. 'There must be another way out!'

She was already running. Nick raced to keep up with her. The flames from the oil lamps guttered, and flared orange light, as they sped past each one.

Callie suddenly heard barking. 'Skatelios!' hissed Nick.

Callie skidded to a halt in front of another doorway. She could see right through to another row of six white columns. The sky beyond flickered with lightning. It illuminated a robed man dragging a snarling, snapping Alsatian dog by its chain. Two further figures in robes were half carrying, half dragging Callie's parents between them. They were lifeless and unresponsive.

'We're too late!' said Nick in dismay.

'They might be drugged,' Callie whispered back. Surely there was no point to all this if her parents were already dead. She edged around one of the columns to get a better view.

She could see a paved platform leading from the end of the temple. It jutted out over granite cliffs like a diving board. In the very centre was a long, flat slab – a sacrificial altar, and it was where her parents were being taken.

Skatelios and Glass Eye deposited them, side by side on the altar. Lobster Tan chained the now yelping dog to an iron ring at the foot of the altar. Then the three men retreated backwards down the platform and knelt, with their faces pressed against the cold, dark stone.

'What are they waiting for?' whispered Nick.

Callie shook her head. 'I don't know.'

A rumble of thunder echoed distantly, and the clouds

momentarily glittered at the edges, as they absorbed sheet lightning.

Skatelios, Lobster Tan Man and Glass Eye stood up and started walking slowly back into the temple.

'Quick!' Callie dragged Nick behind the great temple door where they wouldn't be seen. She tried to stop breathing as she heard Skatelios, Glass Eye and Lobster Tan's footsteps going past. They were so close she could smell Glass Eye's odorous sweat. When the sound had receded away completely, she put a finger to her lips and pointed around the side of the door.

She crept outside and broke into a run, speeding down the paved platform to the altar at the end. 'Mum... Dad... MUM! DAD!'

She saw her mum's chest move slightly. 'It's all right, Nick.' She was reassuring herself as much as Nick. 'They're breathing.'

Nick answered with a sob of relief.

Skatelios was barking on the end of his chain. Not angry, vicious barking as before, but excitement at seeing Nick.

'Shhhh!' Nick told him desperately. 'Shhhh!' He hugged him and started unfastening the chain. The instant the chain was off, Skatelios shot away, as fast as his paws could carry him.

Nick started to say something.

A great roar sounded from the temple. It was a sound that neither of them had wanted to hear again, least of all this close. Barely a human sound; something terrible, unnatural and primeval. Callie spun round to see what it was, what was about to issue from the temple.

There was a another loud cry, somewhere between a roar and a bellow, and it emerged, dragging a heavy sword. *IT WAS A MONSTER WITH THE BODY OF A MAN AND THE HEAD OF A LION.*

Callie gasped. Its head was huge and golden with glowing, horrific eyes, its human muscles were bulging and knotted.

Skatelios and his men had unleashed the Leonotaur. Callie could see their robed figures escaping back down the hillside in the light of the flaming torches.

She felt something digging painfully into her wrist, and realised it was Nick's fingernails. He was gripping her, trying to drag her away. His face was screwed up in terror, and he was shaking all over – or was that her?

The Leonotaur looked round before fixing its amber gaze on the altar. It bellowed once more, wielding the massive sword.

Callie's mind was in meltdown. This couldn't be real. This was a creature from myth! But it *was* real. She could see it. She could hear it! Had some insane priesthood been keeping this *thing* alive through the centuries, chained in the underworld, secretly feeding it sacrifices? Did the priests all wear the lion tattoo?

In the fresco Callie had seen in the museum, four warriors had been fighting the Leonotaur. Had that been a depiction of a real event? Had they really captured it?

'Dad! Wake up!' Nick was shaking their dad maniacally. 'DAAAAAD!'

The Leonotaur had stepped onto the platform. There would be no way past it. It was as wide as the platform itself. Silhouetted against the storm clouds, it continued walking, one deliberate step at a time.

Callie gazed at her parents' faces, peaceful in sleep. It had to be her then. She smiled thinly at Nick. Then, with a scream of despair, and forlorn hope, she sprang at the monster. She *yelled* heroically at it and avoided the slash of its sword, digging her nails into its human flesh, scratching like a lioness. Her nails produced trickles of blood. The Leonotaur roared in outrage. The stench from its gaping mouth was rank. But it brought the sword up, two-handed above its head to strike down with the point into the top of Callie's spine and cripple her before the 'kill'. But it turned aside before striking.

Nick had picked up Skatelios's dog chain and was using it to whip the monster's back. The creature bellowed and spun, flinging both Callie and Nick to the ground. It turned the point of the blade on Nick. Nick screamed. But Skatelios landed on the monster's back, barking and snarling, and savaging its shoulders and neck without mercy. Blood began to pour in crimson rivers down the Leonotaur's chest. It dropped its sword and screamed.

Callie gaped at the creature's lion head. It was a human scream! How could it produce a human scream? Her mind reeled and she thought back. How many men had she seen running down the hill to the mansion? She couldn't be certain. She'd only seen a glimpse of priests' robes in the torchlight.

Gaping wounds in his flesh, the monster had thrown Skatelios off, and recovered its sword.

Callie dashed forward, and tore at the monster's head. It was a MASK and it fell to the stone platform! There was a man beneath the mask! No lion-headed monster, just an ordinary one: Georgiou Skatelios!

Without the mask he looked more terrifying than before, his face distorted with hatred and insanity. 'I WILL KILL HER! I WILL KILL HER!'

He raised the sword above his head and Callie staggered back defenceless.

In the split second before the sword punctured her heart, a sheet of lightning illuminated the entire hillside. Skatelios looked stricken. He burbled something. He was looking directly at Callie and Nick. 'Princess...Electra? King... Akanon?' Then he stared past them, and stumbled back, holding up his hands to shield his face. 'Princess, King – I did not know!'

As he retreated there was nowhere to go. The platform disappeared in a sheer drop on either side. Skatelios tumbled backwards with terror in his bloodshot, insane eyes. He smashed from rock to rock all the way to the ragged ground below.

As Callie turned away from his sickening fall she saw it too. The temple was filled with Mycenaean warriors, spectacular in helmets and armour. King Akanon's army had returned from the tomb to save them.

Then in another flash of lightning she saw she was deceived. They weren't warriors at all. They were the Theltan police, carrying shields and wearing body armour. Skatelios thought he'd seen King Akanon's army, and Skatelios had died.

Callie took one last look down at the mangled remains of the last Mycenaean, and ran to her parents...

22
FISHED FROM THE SEA

'Princess Electra...Princess Electra...'

The Princess hardly dare lift her eyes. She was kneeling with her face buried in her hands. The Leonotaur – half man, half lion – was speaking to her.

'Princess?'

Soft, gentle hands raised her face.

'Your prayer has been heard by the Gods.'

A face swam hazily before Princess Electra's eyes. Not that of a lion?

'But you're a man!'

He was older than her by some forty summers.

'I am the Lion Priest, appointed by your brother, the king Akanon.'

He gestured at a great lion's head mask, discarded on the marble floor.

'Then there is no Leonotaur,' said Princess Electra dully.

'There is for those who believe,' said the Lion Priest. 'And all with courage are part lion.'

'What is to become of me? Our people will think I failed to give my prayer and myself to the Leonotaur, if I return.'

The Lion Priest placed his hand softly on her shoulder.

'You will not leave the lair of the Leonotaur, my Princess.'

Princess Electra was trembling from head to toe. She

257

must sacrifice herself after all. Then the Lion Priest went on: 'You are to become one of the exalted priestesses.'

'But they are chosen by the Gods,' said Princess Electra, in astonishment.

'As you have been, Princess, by your sacrifice and by your courage.' He smiled. 'Though, in time, if you wish to leave, you will not be denied.'

'What of my brother? What of King Akanon?'

'The Gods are the Gods, child. They will help him if they will.'

Princess Electra nodded, acceptingly...

They were sitting beside the pool at Villa Limani. Their parents were being questioned inside by the police.

'He thought he'd seen the Mycenaean army, and imagined you to be King Akanon and Princess Electra, returned from the grave,' said Khrisous. 'He'd been looking at ancient paintings of the King and Princess only hours before.'

Callie opened her mouth to ask a question, but Khrisous anticipated it.

'James Spearman said he'd downloaded images from your mobile phone onto Skatelios's computer.'

Nick screwed up his face. 'Who's James Spearman?'

'Lobster Tan Man,' Callie told him.

Khrisous smiled at the name. 'Lobster Tan Man. Yes... According to *Lobster Tan Man*, you both bear a remarkable resemblance to our ancient Mycenaean rulers.'

'Perhaps we've got the same DNA,' said Nick.

'Why did you come to Skatelios Island?' asked Callie.

'We guessed you might have been taken there by Skatelios and his men. Officer Papadopoulos saw you go into the villa but did not see you come out.'

Nick screwed up his face again. 'Who's Officer Papadopoulos?'

This time Callie shrugged.

'Yiannis Papadopoulos,' explained Khrisous. 'He has been watching your villa.'

'Yiannis is police?' spluttered Nick. 'No wonder he's a useless gardener. He's killed half of our plants.'

'But he was working here *before* our parents completed King Akanon's map,' said Callie, in confusion.

'We had received information that a section of the famous map had been sold over the internet to your parents.'

'Oh – that.'

'Whoops!' said Nick.

'At first Officer Papadopoulos thought you might be locked in the Treasury and tried to rescue you.'

'Rescue us!' exploded Nick. 'He only brought the whole of Thelta crashing down on top of us – AND the treasure!'

'Strange. King Akanon's Treasury looked intact when we opened it this morning.'

'WHAT???' Callie and Nick had shouted together.

'Fortunately, Officer Papadopoulos gave up before the chamber collapsed.'

Callie had to stop herself jumping for joy.

'Tell me, is it an English thing, defying adults?' Khrisous went on.

'It's kind of expected,' Nick told him.

'You should not have run away from my office, or again at the waterfront. We were trying to ensure your safety.'

'We didn't think you were going to help us,' said Callie. 'We thought you were working for Skatelios.'

Khrisous looked surprised.

'You were acting like his long lost brother at the police station,' said Nick.

Khrisous slapped his balding forehead, and gave out a great sigh. 'It was unfortunate you should see that. I could prove nothing, and I wanted him to believe I had no further suspicions.'

'Well, you convinced him *and* us,' said Nick.

'What will happen to our parents?' asked Callie.

'They are our primary witnesses against Skatelios, and the other three men who work for him. Their evidence against them all will be crucial. But after they have given their statements, they will be free to carry on their work. You have provided them with many new archaeological sites.'

Callie wondered if she was hearing things. Free to carry on their work?

Khrisous pressed the fingertips of his hands together. 'I believe their crime regarding the stolen clay tablet can be overlooked. Their, or should I say *your*, discoveries will bring great wealth and fame to all of Thelta.'

'We should probably receive a reward then,' said Nick optimistically.

Callie kicked him.

'Did I tell you I have four children of my own?' asked Khrisous, suddenly changing the subject.

'I think you mentioned it,' said Nick.

'Where are we going?' Callie and Nick were in Manolis's little red and yellow boat, on an inky blue sea, under a waning moon.

'It's a surprise,' replied Manolis, with his usual friendly smile.

Callie's parents hadn't even *tried* to stop them coming out with Manolis. After the last few days they'd decided they could take care of themselves. They hadn't even said what time they had to be back! It would never last.

'The newspaper said your parents are to receive a reward,' said Manolis, piloting the boat south along the coastline; steering by the twinkling lights of the harbours.

'That was my idea,' said Nick. 'King Akanon's treasure must be worth millions!'

Nick had been calculating for the last three days, since Skatelios had fallen from his own cliff, just how much King Akanon's treasure was worth. He was currently speculating they should now be worth more than Bill Gates.

'The reward's only worth about one of King Akanon's toes,' he complained.

Callie stifled a laugh.

'One of King Akanon's toes?' Manolis looked baffled.

'We saw a gigantic golden statue of King Akanon underwater,' explained Callie.

'And his big toe was about *this* big!' added Nick, demonstrating something the size of a football with his hands.

'The reward won't make them rich,' Callie said. 'But at least they can pay off all their debts. In the meantime they seem to have gone off treasure hunting. They said that last week had made them realise they already had all the treasure they needed. Me and Nick.'

Nick rolled his eyes. 'At least we've still got this,' he said, producing a massive bundle of euros in an elastic band.

'Nick! I keep telling you to give that back!'

Nick pulled a face. 'I will!'

'Well, do it while there's some left, will you.'

'All right! All right! Don't go on, else I won't keep saving your life next time.'

'Next time? Forget it!' Callie gave him a playful punch. Nick grinned broadly.

'Here we are,' Manolis announced, starting to guide the boat into a dark shoreline.

'Here we are *where*?' asked Callie.

'We must wait on the beach,' said Manolis, ignoring the question. 'And we can't use torches. It confuses them.'

'Confuses who?' said Callie and Nick together, utterly mystified...

It seemed hours, but for the first time in days they were

in no hurry, then Manolis was whispering, 'Look, look! Here's the first one!'

A stone's throw away, a green, loggerhead turtle was making its way ashore to lay its eggs. It was digging its flippers into the sand to propel itself forward a bit at a time as if trying to swim through sand.

'Does it remind you of Callie swimming?' asked Nick, and laughed so hard it was a wonder the turtle didn't turn round and head straight back into the sea.

'Oh ha ha ha.' Callie tucked herself up in one of Manolis's boat blankets contentedly. She was soon asleep and far away.

It was a fine palace, worthy of Priam, the King of Troy.

Callie saw that King Akanon was grown to a young man, taller and stronger, with a face which was breathtakingly beautiful. He was pacing up and down in the city's gardens.

Laomedon, a prince of Troy, interrupted him.

'Akanon! Cease this endless pacing! Calm yourself, Greek king.'

'Calm myself!' Akanon's voice was deep and resonant. 'I am more afraid today than on any other day since I was fished from the Aegean Sea. This day I am to marry Princess Dreiseus, the very person who fished me out!'

'I know!' Laomedon gave King Akanon a friendly thump on the back. 'And a strange fish, Princess Dreiseus landed indeed — one who does not wish to marry her.'

Callie saw King Akanon's worried expression change instantly to one of earnest love.

'But I do wish to marry her. With all my heart,' he said fervently. 'Dreiseus suffered King Priam's wrath for saving the life of a Mycenaean – a Mycenaean king at that, who had sailed across the ocean to make war on him!'

'Yes, yes,' said Laomedon impatiently. 'And since that day you and she have been parted rarely. She would not even trust your safety to us, her own kinsmen, at first!'

'Until I won you over,' grinned King Akanon. 'Even you, great Laomedon, Champion of the Trojans.'

Prince Laomedon's strong face set. 'Do not be so certain, King of Thelta. Merely because you saved your warriors from a sinking ship... Merely because you asked for death rather than join our army against your own... Merely because you ride a horse like the very gods...'

King Akanon broke into a long, rich laugh, and Laomedon joined him.

'Now, come Akanon. WE are late.'

Akanon nodded. 'I am afraid no longer.'

'Good. There is not a man in all of Troy who does not love Princess Dreiseus, AND SHE LOVES YOU! So stay with her in Troy and be happy.'

And Callie knew that he had.